PRAISE FOR
JAIMIE ENGLE

Amazon #1 New Release
L. Ron Hubbard Writers of the Future Award

BRAG Medallion Honoree Award
Top Ten Book of 2014 Kid Lit Reviews

"…the world Engle has created in this novel is an intriguing one, equal parts familiar and fantastic." *Kirkus Reviews*

"…belongs on your bookshelf - young or old - right along with Tolkien and Grimm." –Amazon.com

"I did not want to leave until the last page was turned." –Kid Lit Reviews

"…the same kind of universe you might meet Captain Malcolm Reynolds or Luke Skywalker in." –The Story Sanctuary Reviews

"Jaimie Engle brings "The Dredge" to an exciting, unexpected, and ultimately satisfying ending." –Third Flatiron Editor

BOOKS BY JAIMIE ENGLE

FICTION

Clifton Chase and the Arrow of Light, Coloring Book
Condensed version of the novel with pictures to color

The Dredge
Supernatural gifts are sought through deception in a future world

Dreadlands: Wolf Moon
A Viking boy must face shifting wolves or become their prey

The Toilet Papers: Places to Go, While you Go
Short story collection of humor, horror, and historical for adults 16+

The Toilet Papers, Jr.
Short story colleciion of humor, horror, & fairy tales

Metal Mouth
A girl's braces transmit a boy's voice after being struck by lightning

NON-FICTION

Clifton Chase and the Arrow of Light Teacher Guide
Teacher Curriculum Guide to use with the novel

Write a Book that Doesn't Suck (Indie Series Book #2)
A No-Nonsense Guide to Writing Epic Fiction

How to Publish Your Book (Indie Series Book #1)
A step-by-step ebook to get your book published! (Amazon #1)

Visit the author at thewriteengle.com.

Clifton Chase
and the
Arrow of Light

Jaimie Engle

Enjoy the adventure !

INtense Publications
www.intensepublications.com

INtense Publications

Paperback ISBN: 978-1-947796-29-4

Clifton Chase and the Arrow of Light

Copyright © 2013 Jaimie Engle

This is a work of fiction. Names, characters, places and incidents are either the product of the author's imagination or are used fictitiously and any resemblance to actual persons, living or dead, business establishments, events or locales is entirely coincidental.

This edition published by arrangement with INtense Publications LLC. The opinions expressed by the author are not necessarily those of INtense Publications LLC.

Cover design © 2015 Philip Benjamin of Benjamin Studios

Cover art & interior illustrations © 2013 Debbie Johnson

www.INtensePublications.com

Printed in U.S.A.

In memory of Sam and Marie Dibella.
FOR ALL THE BOOKS

Chapter One
The Boy and the Arrow

T
he thought that this was a brainless thing to do hadn't crossed his mind until now. He fumbled to fit his bow, his fingers like gelatin, as classmates lined up beside him in Wickham Park. The rest of the seventh graders gathered around to see who would win the bet between Clifton Chase and the new kid, Ryan Rivales. The instructor counted down the seconds from his stopwatch, and Clifton swiveled around to see if a certain pair of green eyes watched him. Yup. Even Ava Harrington had come to see.

"Ready…" the instructor said.

As sweat stung his eyes, Clifton remembered why he'd taken the bet. It was this arrow. He'd found it mysteriously in his closet, and then it lit up for a split second. At least he thought it had. It seemed so otherworldly at the time, and when Ryan started in on him, the only thing he could think to do was show that kid up.

"Take aim…" the instructor continued.

Now he wasn't sure.

He pulled the notched arrow back. He had one chance, a single-shot test for precision, straight to the bullseye or be the closest shot. Ryan wagered his sleek emerald green binary compound bow, but they both knew this bet was not about the antique arrow or the slick bow. It was for bragging rights, for pecking order.

For making it through middle school as king.

"Loose!"

On command, arrows arced through the air, landing on the targets or the wooden posts they were nailed to. Some struck the 3D molded deer, which now resembled a porcupine. A few arrows passed their marks altogether, landing out of sight in the tall grasses of the hilly dunes. 'The Hinterland' as it had been nicknamed. And that's where Clifton's arrow went.

"Archers… Halt!" the instructor shouted. "The range is now cold. You may retrieve your arrows."

Clifton lifted his backpack and stepped onto the range with the others.

"What happened?" Ava asked. "You usually have perfect aim."

Clifton's hands went clammy whenever she came around. It hadn't always been that way, just recently. "Yeah, well, I guess that crappy arrow wasn't as good as Ryan thought it was."

"Why'd you make that bet with him? Didn't you say you found that thing in your garage or something?"

"My closet, actually." Sunlight brightened her eyes, and he stared a moment longer than he'd meant to.

"Well, it seems weird for you. I don't get it."

"There's not much to get, Ava,"

"Except my arrow," said Ryan as he neared them. "Nice shot, by the way." He snickered, and the few kids who'd tagged behind him laughed.

"Wasn't my fault," Clifton said. "I'd never shot it before."

"Doesn't matter now. I won the bet. My arrow didn't even need to land near the bull's eye, just on the target."

More laughter erupted, and Clifton turned away.

Ryan shoved him. "Where you going, Chase?"

Clifton did a one-eighty. "Going to get that worthless arrow you won. Must feel good to know your shot beat an antique."

Ryan's smile dropped. "My shot," he said in a clipped tone, "beat your shot. Now go find my arrow and hand it over."

Clifton's hands balled into fists as he left the circle to reach the edge of The Hinterland. Ava followed.

"I can't believe what a jerk that guy is," Clifton said. "Can you believe how epic he thinks he is? Like he's the greatest archer of all times. *Robin Hood Rivales.*"

Ava's hands perched on her hips. "You're the one that tried convincing him your arrow was something special when you knew it wasn't. Seems like maybe Ryan's not the one being the jerk. See you later, Clifton."

Clifton lowered his head, defeated. He'd lost the arrow, lost the compound bow, lost his dignity, and Ava thought he was a jerk. Now, he had to trudge through The Hinterland, looking for the ridiculous arrow that started it all. He swore under his breath and headed up the dune.

Across the way, Juan Sanchez, another victim of inaccuracy, scanned the brush facedown like Clifton. He was about to suggest they join forces when something sunk through his sock into his ankle. Sandspurs. He'd run through a whole patch and took a few minutes to pick them off, which hurt his fingers as much as his ankles. As he avoided a red ant pile, he almost tripped on a root that jutted up like a step.

And still, he hadn't found his arrow.

About to give up and turn back, he glimpsed something copper-colored in the tall brush up ahead. Clifton spread back the grass to reveal the fletching. Were the feathers swaying? Nah, they couldn't be. There wasn't even a breeze. Then, he remembered how the shaft had glowed in his bedroom. No, way. This arrow was as plain as any other. And what did it matter?

It wasn't his anymore.

He grabbed the arrow, and as soon as he touched it, a wave of dizziness passed over him while a CRACK filled the air. Clifton stood, turned to head back toward the range, but froze. He was standing in the middle of an open field covered in yellow flowers that rolled like carpet into the base of the surrounding snow-capped mountains.

The Hinterland was gone, replaced with a shimmer in the air like heat off a highway. And with a sudden sweat, he realized that Wickham Park was gone too.

Chapter Two
Dwarfed

"Hello?" Clifton yelled. "Is there anybody here?"

A group of birds, startled by his voice, shot out of the grass, and Clifton jumped. The arrow grew warm, then so hot he dropped it to the ground and blew against his palm. The shaft glowed as it had in his bedroom; only this time, it didn't burn out.

"I'm having a dream," Clifton said, taking a step back. "A very vivid dream."

Clifton nudged it with the toe of his sneaker, and the arrow started to rumble, moving the grass as it slowly turned like the hand of a clock. Once it had shimmied forty-five-degrees, it stopped moving, the tip pointing toward a forest far in the distance.

"Apparently, a glowing arrow wants me to head that way," Clifton said.

The arrow glowed intensely for a few seconds then faded back to plain wood.

"I'll take that as a yes."

The fletching moved again, reminding Clifton of the way his little brother Pierce would wiggle his fingers in the air when he wanted to be picked up. "Does this arrow want me to pick it up?" he said. Again, the shaft glowed brightly then went cold. "Great. I'm communicating with a magical arrow."

He reached for it, surprised to find that the shaft had cooled, and placed the arrow in his backpack. Somehow it fit; the fletching, slipping inside the shaft, like the arrow was retractable.

"I'm closing the zipper now," Clifton warned as if the arrow understood him. "This is too weird." He slung his backpack onto his shoulders and headed through the flowers toward the forest.

It stayed quiet for some time, with nothing but his breathing and a cool breeze that occasionally swept past. A flock of geese flew overhead. He stopped to watch them, then kept walking. "Man, it sure is hot for a dream. I don't ever remember sweating in my sleep. I hope I'm not getting sick."

The flowers cleared as he moved along, and now, he was walking through the green grass. "Maybe I hit my head on that oak," he said. "That's it. I must be passed out from a concussion in Wickham Park and this is all in my head." He smiled at the thought, but then, his smile faded. "Only, it doesn't feel like it's in my head. The sun is hot, and my feet hurt."

As the grass thinned into clumpy patches, a dirt pathway formed between the spaces. "Remember, Clifton; this is a dream. It's all in your head," he told himself as he trudged along, moving closer to the tree-line of the forest.

Ahead, a patch of blackberries caught his eye, right off the path. He sat down to rest for a while, popping berries in his mouth until he had tasted enough. This dream wasn't so bad after all until a wolf howled in the distance. The animal noises were changing, the awakening of nocturnal creatures that gave Clifton the chills. He got back on the path and didn't stop until he reached the tree-line of tall firs.

He had read many stories about children getting lost in the woods, walking for hours, but always arriving back where they had started. Considering he was pretty much stuck in this dream that he couldn't wake up from, Clifton had no choice but to follow the dirt path into the woods. So, he did.

A canopy of oaks twisted skyward in an odd spiral pattern. Sunlight sifted in streams through the branches. An occasional breeze rattled the high leaves above Clifton, starting in the distance and chasing across the treetops. Other than the wind, the still woods seemed eerily quiet. No birds or squirrels. No bugs. No life at all as he pressed deeper, like walking through a painting rather than through real life.

Then, a branch snapped, and Clifton stiffened.

He scanned the forest but found nothing. With a deep breath, he quickened his pace along the path, as another snap whipped him around. "Hello?"

Nothing moved.

Except for Clifton, who ran for his life, backpack slamming against his back with each stride. Why wasn't he waking up? This dream had turned into a nightmare.

With a sudden jolt from behind, someone pushed Clifton to the ground and knocked the wind out of him. He scrambled to get up, but whoever shoved him was sitting on his back to keep him down.

"Be still, child. I wish you no harm."

"Get off me!"

"Quiet!" The man pressed Clifton's head into the dirt. "Now, I will release you if you promise to keep quiet."

Clifton nodded and said, "I promise," which came out as "I bomis."

After a few moments, the man removed his hand from Clifton's head and rolled off his back. Clifton quickly pushed to his feet and turned around. Standing before him was a man no more than four feet tall, resembling a dwarf—the kind Clifton read about in storybooks, with a bulbous nose, bushy red eyebrows, and a wispy, red beard.

"Where is the arrow?" the dwarf asked.

Heat flashed through Clifton's body, and he knew his face

reddened. "I don't know what you're talking about."

The dwarf shot forward, grabbing him by the shirt. "Dontcha be lyin' to me, boy. I know you have the arrow. Where is it?"

Clifton's heart raced. "It's in my backpack."

The little man's blue eyes narrowed. Clifton stared back, afraid to breathe. "We must move quickly," the dwarf said, releasing his grip.

"Why?"

"It's not safe here." He veered into the darkening woods, leaving the dirt path behind.

Clifton watched him go, wondering if he should follow the aggressive little man.

The dwarf turned. "Now, Clifton."

Clifton took a step back. "How do you know my name?"

"There's no time to explain. Ya must trust me."

Clifton felt the ground spin as he stood, afraid to move forward, afraid to press back. He thought he might pass out. Then he remembered that he already had. "It's all in your head," he whispered to himself.

The dwarf backpedaled. "I know this must be strange fer ya, boy."

"You have no idea."

"All yer questions will be answered in good time. I promise. But right now, we need to get out of the woods."

"Why?" Clifton asked again.

"Because," the dwarf said. "*He* knows yer here."

Chapter Three

Stew

Off the beaten path, fallen branches, and leaves littered the forest floor. Clifton did his best to not stumble in the growing darkness, struggling to keep up with the little man who bounded several strides ahead.

"Who knows I'm here?" Clifton asked, between breaths.

The dwarf did not answer.

"I said...who knows I'm here?"

The dwarf turned sharply, and Clifton hopped on his toes to catch his weight before barreling into the little man.

"Quiet, boy," he said, his brows scrunched. "There are eyes all over this forest. Keep quiet and keep moving."

Clifton did as he was told, staying close to the dwarf and not saying another word. The branches above them rattled. An owl perched on the bough, the first living creature Clifton had seen in the forest besides the dwarf. It stared at him, unblinking, its head turning mechanically.

There are eyes all over this forest.

A shiver crawled across Clifton's skin. The owl spread its wings and flew, gliding toward him. Clifton ducked, missing its sharp talons but bumping into the dwarf, who turned. Clifton pointed to where the owl had been, but it was gone.

The dwarf rolled his eyes. "Over here, lad."

Behind a dense patch of green leaves and branches, smoke billowed in gray puffs. The dwarf pulled aside some hanging vines and disappeared. Clifton followed. A cottage with a straw-thatched roof lay hidden behind the foliage and a pebbled pathway lined by an herb garden led to the entranceway. The lingering scent of dill hung on the air.

"Welcome to me home," the dwarf said, pushing open the wooden door.

Clifton stepped into the warm foyer greeted by the scent of stewing meat and vegetables. His mouth watered. The dwarf led Clifton down a hallway lined by dark brown wood paneling, etched with vines budding flowers that climbed toward a leaf border. Candles wedged in brass stands sat on cluttered tables and small trunks all over the cottage. The hall ended at the kitchen, where a woman faced a brick fireplace. Her hair was the same shade of wild red as the man's, and her figure was equally as stout. She stirred a wooden spoon in a cauldron that hung over the flame.

"Yer back," she said, wiping her hands on her apron. "Is this the boy?" She scooted toward them.

"Of course, it's the boy," the dwarf barked.

"Ya must be famished," she said, eyeing Clifton up and down. "Why, yer nothing but skin and bones."

"Ya don't think I can find a boy out in these woods?"

"Come. Sit," the woman said, ignoring the dwarf. She led Clifton to a chair at the block table in the center of the room. "Here. Have some bread."

Clifton set his backpack on the floor and took a seat. His back ached from the hours of hiking, and the hard chair did nothing to make it better. The woman sliced dark bread from a loaf on the table and handed a piece to Clifton. Honey and golden wheat coated his tongue, and his eyes closed. "It's so good," he said, his words garbled by bread.

"More where that came from," she said, returning to the stew.

The dwarf stared at his empty plate, grunted, and ripped a chunk of bread from the loaf. "Now, show me the arrow."

Clifton shoveled in bread, bent over, and grabbed the arrow from his backpack. He almost choked as it grew to its regular size before his eyes. The dwarf snatched it, a crooked little smile crossing his face. His fingers passed through the barbs of the fletching, then continued smoothly down the shaft. With wide eyes, the woman joined the man, fixated on the arrow.

"That's really it, ain't it?" she asked.

The dwarf didn't answer, smacking bread between his molars, sliding his fingers across the arrow's diamond-like tip.

"What is it?" Clifton asked.

The man looked up, his expression surprised as if he had forgotten Clifton was sitting there. "Let's eat first. Wife?"

Scurrying back to the cauldron, the woman ladled stew into clay bowls. She placed one before each of them, and the three devoured gamey stew, with thick carrots and new potatoes. They ate in silence except for the slurping sounds made by the dwarf and his wife as they gulped down every last drop. Clifton might've even licked the bowl clean if he hadn't been taught any better. Even in his dreams, he worried about what his mom might think. And though he'd never tell his mother this, that stew was the most delicious meal he could ever remember eating.

Chapter Four
Sleep

"Have ya had enough?" the woman asked.

Clifton rubbed his stomach. "Yes, ma'am. I'm stuffed."

"Should be. After two bowls," the dwarf said.

"He's a growing boy. Leave him alone."

"That's less supper for me on the morrow."

The woman cleared the bowls and spoons, loading them into a large pan. "Help me with the door, Love."

The dwarf stood and shuffled to the front door, saying something to his wife Clifton couldn't overhear. She carried the pan of dishes outside, which he found odd until he scanned the kitchen and found no indoor plumbing. She must have one of those old-fashioned water pumps he had learned about in history class.

After closing the door, the dwarf said, "Come here, lad. Join me in the sitting room. And bring yer pack." He crossed and approached two chairs made from boughs of the oaks Clifton had seen in the forest, held together with twine situated next to a small table near the fireplace. The dwarf sat in the one with curved wood on each side for rocking, and while gently gliding, said, "Sit down, lad. Relax. I ain't gonna bite ya."

Clifton stared at the other chair. It looked like a bunch of toothpicks held together with dental floss. Gingerly, he applied his full weight to the seat and braced. Luckily, the chair held.

The dwarf pulled a slender pipe from his vest pocket, opened an expensive-looking canister on the end table, and stuffed a pinch of tobacco into the chamber. "I bet yer head be full of questions," he said with a smirk.

Clifton scoffed. "That's the understatement of the year."

"Well, what would ya like to know?" he asked, pulling a match from the canister.

Clifton ran his fingers through his hair. "Am I dreaming?"

"Not likely," the dwarf replied. His cream-colored shirt lay opened at his neck, revealing a chest full of curly red hairs.

"Probable concussion."

"What, lad?"

"Never mind. I'll play along. Where am I?"

"Griffon Forest." The dwarf struck the match and touched the flame to the chamber, puffing several times to prime the tobacco. "That's it?"

"Are you kidding me? I have a million questions. Like, who are you? And how did I get here—who's after me? And what's up with that arrow?"

The dwarf blew out a vanilla-tobacco smoke cloud. "Whoa, lad. Slow down. Let's take one question at a time."

"Fine. Who are you?"

"The name is Dane. Dane Englewood, son of Drathco."

"And you're a...dwarf?"

"Aye. So is me wife, Liv."

"So where am I and what am I doing here? And where is here exactly?

"Again, slow down. Can't be answering six questions at a time."

"How did you know I was here before I did?"

"Let's just say for now that I did."

"That's not helpful, Dane."

"I'll tell ya what," Dane said as he rocked. "Tomorrow, you will meet the ones who sent me. We leave for Flaxton Village after breakfast."

"Wait, someone sent you to find me? Who?"

"You will find out tomorrow. Now, dontcha want to know anything else about me?"

"How far is Flaxton Village far from here? And where is here again?"

Dane blew out smoke. "Thought I told ya that."

Clifton shook his head.

"I see." He cleared his throat. "You, my lad, are in Griffon Forest."

Clifton held his head in his hands. "Not helpful to know what you call places when I don't know where they are. What country am I in?"

"Yer in England, in York to be exact."

"England?" Clifton stood. "I'm sorry, but it sounded like you just said I'm in England. And that couldn't be possible."

"Of course, it's possible, because ya *are* in England."

Clifton took a step back, though he wanted to run away. He wished someone in the real world would slap him or pour gallons of ice water over his head. Something, anything to wake him up. "England? No, it's not true. It can't be true. Oh, God, what if it is true? I have to get out of here." Clifton charged to the front door.

"Clifton, sit down. Sit! Down!"

Clifton stopped short and faced Dane, who had stood and sighed deeply. "Please. Come sit down and let me speak."

Clifton absently rubbed his arms as he mumbled, "I just can't believe this," and trailed back to his chair by the fire. He slumped in his seat, avoiding eye contact, and crossed his arms over his stomach. "Not possible," he said under his breath. He was stuck in this dream, one that felt more and more real by the minute.

Dane rocked in his chair and smoked his pipe, as he said, "The arrow brought ya here. And the man after ya is King Richard the third."

Clifton stared at the fire. "King who the what?"

"King Richard the third, the king of England."

"Well, that's good then." Clifton snickered. "I'm sorry, but isn't he dead?"

Dane stopped rocking. The two stared at each other as the front door opened, and Liv entered carrying the empty bin.

"I'm back," she sang. "How are ya boys getting on?" She paused, the tension in the air thick. "Oh," she said before clearing her throat. "I best leave ya two alone, then." She set the bin down and left the room, humming.

"This is ridiculous," Clifton said. "You don't honestly expect me to believe any of this, do you?"

"I don't expect this to be easy for ya, Clifton, but ya have to believe it 'cause it's truth. Tomorrow you will meet a boy in Flaxton who will have more of the answers ya seek. It is his arrow which you carry."

"Then why do I have it?" Clifton asked, glaring at the dwarf. "If it belongs to him? How did I get it?"

Dane shrugged. "I dunno."

"Well, what happens to me when he gets his arrow back?"

"I dunno," Dane said.

"Jeez, Dane. Aren't you supposed to have all the answers?"

Dane faced the fire to enjoy his pipe, and Clifton threw his hands into the air. They sat in silence as the fire warmed them for several minutes, Dane smoking his tobacco pipe, Clifton muttering his disbelief as he tried to pinch himself awake.

Liv poked her head back into the room. "Clifton, yer chambers be ready." She smiled. It was a soft smile, full of warmth and caring. It reminded him of his mother, who he suddenly missed very much.

He wished he'd never found that trouble-making arrow.

"Let's call it a night then, shall we?" Dane said standing. "We have quite a long journey set for us next morrow. And Clifton?"

Clifton looked at Dane, who simply grinned, then shifted down the hall and out of the cottage without a word.

What was that all about?

"This way," Liv said.

She nodded down the hall that led to the opposite end of the cottage, her hands clasped at her chest. Grabbing the arrow and his backpack, Clifton followed her, shuffling his feet loudly across the floor. His small candlelit room contained a single bed, nightstand, and a chair with a dragon painted on the spine.

"Good-night," Liv said sweetly, closing the door behind her.

Clifton stood for a moment in the silent room. His head hurt. His brain spun. He peered out the small window at a large white moon, bleached grass, and trees he did not recognize.

Where was he?

Sitting on the edge of the bed, he slid off his shoes and wet socks, then peeled out of his dirty clothes. The down comforter warmed him as he lay on his back, staring at the ceiling. How could this all be a dream? But it had to be a dream. In the morning, he would wake up in his own room, in his own bed, and all of this would disappear. He lay in the dark unconvinced for some time. And those were the last thoughts he remembered.

Chapter Five
Waking

C lifton opened his eyes to the shrill cock-a-doodle-doo of someone's rooster alarm. It was still dark out. Wasn't it Sunday? Who set their alarm so early? Come to think of it, no one in his house had a rooster alarm. And that bird sounded real. He looked around, a pile of clothes on a painted chair, a water bowl, a hand towel...

This was not his room.

He stood to peek outside the makeshift window. A forest, not a neighborhood. No Florida palms. No swimming pool.

He was still dreaming.

Pivoting, he stepped too fast, tripped on the leg of the bed, and braced his fall with the edge of the water bowl. Water swooshed out onto his clothes piled beneath him. "Perfect," he said.

He opened the bedroom door that creaked to give away his position and peered out to an empty hall — no one in sight. With what was left in the bowl, he washed his face and dried off with the soft towel, then sat on the edge of the bed for some time. He must have a really bad concussion for this dream to last so long. He hoped he wasn't dying in the real world or in a coma or something. His head fell into his palms and tears welled in his eyes. Then, his opened backpack started to shake like popcorn when it really gets going.

The arrow.

"What do you want?" he asked

The arrow glowed brightly for several minutes, the diamond-point in line with the pile of clothes on the chair, and then went dark and still. Like before. Disgusted, Clifton kicked his backpack and flopped down on the bed with a sigh.

How was he supposed to get out of this mess?

From out back, muffled voices, which sounded like the dwarves', drifted in. He couldn't see them when he poked his head out the window. He'd have to go out there. He looked to the chair, where the clothes were neatly folded, cloth pants, without buttons or a zipper, and a long-sleeved tunic.

"What in the world?" He pulled the cloth pants up to his waist before letting go. They dropped to his ankles. "How am I supposed to wear these?"

Clifton turned the tunic, for a way to attach it to the pants, but found nothing. Finally, two straps on the floor decidedly became pins that held the tunic to the pants in an awkward ensemble. He didn't have a mirror but figured he looked as ridiculous as he felt. After lacing up the snug-fitting hide boots, he stepped outside of the bedroom. "Hello?"

No one responded. Clifton crept back to the now-empty sitting area, kitchen, and dining room, where fresh candles burned in brass holders, and a fire crackled beneath the large black cauldron. Opening the front door, Clifton shouted, "Hello?"

"Out here, lad," Dane called, from around back.

Clifton breathed in the cool morning air as he strolled along the cottage to the backyard. Despite all the trouble, he smiled at the beauty of his surroundings.

"Good morrow," Dane said, from the doorway of a wooden shed. "Those clothes be much more fitting than the garments ya showed up in."

"Yeah, it took me a hot minute," Clifton answered. The dwarf gave him a funny look, and Clifton quickly added, "What's going on out here?"

With a large butcher knife in one hand, Dane held pieces of dried meat in the other. "Hope yer hungry."

"Very." Clifton shook his matted hair and took in a breath to speak before the dwarf cut him off.

"I know yer still full of questions, but let's get some food in our bellies before we talk. Now, be a good lad and see if Liv needs a hand."

He motioned across the yard to a large wooden chicken coop on stilts. The sides were uniform sticks tied together with twine, making the birds look like they were in a tiny prison. Clifton wondered if this was where the phrase *flew the coop* came from, as he imagined all the chickens planning a midnight escape. Liv exited the enclosure, her apron upturned, the top of her hair brushing the inside of the low-shingled roof.

"Do you need some help?" Clifton asked.

Liv smiled. "Well, now. Ain't you quite the gentleman? Follow me." She passed him, heading toward the back of the cottage. As she approached Dane, she said in a loud voice, "Could be showing some of yer good manners to me husband."

Dane glowered. Liv smiled. "Open the back door, Love," she told Clifton.

He opened it and followed her into the kitchen. She leaned over the block table, gently lowering the brown eggs from her apron. Grabbing a pan, she placed it on the hot bricks inside the fire.

The back door opened, and Dane entered. "Bringing home the bacon," he said, laying down the salt-cured slices.

"Like a good man," Liv said, wrapping her arms around him.

Dane took a seat while Liv paid attention to the steaming cauldron beside the pan. "Clifton, get your pack."

He went to his room and grabbed his backpack, then sat at the table. Dane wedged cheese, bread, and cured meat into a large sack with a shoulder strap. Liv set a clay cup filled with a froth covered drink before Clifton. It reminded him of cappuccino.

He blew the foam to the edge and sipped the hot drink. Tastes of black licorice, sugar, and cream danced on his taste buds. "This is delicious. What is it?"

"I call it Dropwater," Liv said. "It'll get ya going with a start. And keep you going, all the way to Flaxton."

"It's amazing," Clifton said, his lip covered in a froth mustache.

"Made with black licorice root from me own garden," she bragged, cracking eggs into the hot pan and frying bacon beside them.

Dane cleared his throat.

"Sorry, Love," Liv said, carrying over a second clay cup for her husband.

He took the Dropwater and swallowed a gulp. He didn't seem to mind the heat. Clifton fiddled with the breadboard, tapped his fingers on the table, and counted the candles in the room. Finally, he couldn't take it anymore. "Okay. So I'm in England. And some magical arrow brought me here. That's what you're telling me, right?"

"That's right," Dane said.

"And a beautiful time of year to be here," Liv added with a dreamy smile.

"How did I get here?"

"The arrow."

"Right. The arrow. Funny thing about that arrow. Did you know it glows? And it moves, too. Actually, I've even seen the feathers sway when there isn't any breeze."

"Aye, lad. I know."

"Well, if you know so much, then tell me what's going on."

Liv set plates of steaming eggs, toast, and bacon in front of them and poured Dane more hot Dropwater. "Go on," she said. "Eat up."

Dane lifted his toast and sank it into the runny yolks. "Flaxton Village is half a day's journey from here. Now is not the time to talk, but to eat. So, eat hearty, and eat fast."

"No," Clifton said, pounding his fists so hard on the table that the clay cups bounced. "I want answers."

Dane looked up from his meal into Clifton's firm face. The dwarf set his toast on the edge of his plate and leaned back in his seat. Taking a deep breath, he said, "Clifton, have ya ever had a piece of cake so delicious ya thought you could eat the whole cake?"

"A piece of cake?" Clifton stared at him as if he was crazy. "What are you talking about?"

"Tell me. What would happen if ya ate the whole cake?"

Clifton threw his hands up in the air. "I don't know. I'd get sick."

"Exactly," Dane said, snapping his fingers. "Cause too much of something, even a great thing, is never a good thing. Understand?"

Clifton looked at him, the analogy lost.

"What yer asking me to tell ya is too much to handle all at once. Trust me. You will have yer answers. But in the right time."

Clifton realized there wasn't much he could do but wait, as he picked up a piece of bacon and took a bite. "So, these boys, the ones in Flaxton, are they cool?"

"Cool?"

"Yeah, you know. Are they nice?"

The dwarf went back to his meal, and Clifton took that as a sign to shut up and eat. So, he did. He paid attention instead to the flavor of the savory bacon, which tasted like it had been seeped in salty-sweet maple syrup. And the eggs, fresh hen eggs, better than any from back home. Dream or no dream, the food was amazing.

They finished breakfast and cleaned up. Dane packed the remaining items for the journey while Liv kept adding more to his sack. Clifton smiled. They could almost be sweet. The three stepped outside, and Clifton faced Liv who stood in the entranceway.

"Thanks for letting me stay," he said. "And for the great meals. You sure are a good cook."

Liv took him by the hands and squeezed. "You be careful, child. And do what the dwarf tells ya to."

"I will," he said and started down the path. "Thanks again!"

"Ya ready, lad?" Dane asked.

"Let's do this."

When they reached the foliage camouflaging the cottage, Liv yelled, "Dwarf!" Dane and Clifton both turned back. "Ya take good care of that boy."

"I know, woman. I don't need ya advising me."

"And, ya take good care of yerself, too, Love."

"Aye, Milady." They held a longing gaze before Dane passed through the hanging limbs and out of sight. Clifton smiled at Liv, who waved from the doorway, her red hair shining in the sun, then pushed the branches aside and stepped back into Griffon Forest.

Chapter Six

Journey

G riffon Forest looked nothing like it had the night before.
Birds flew. Squirrels gathered nuts. The winding trees,
once spiraling into darkness, now welcomed streams of
bright light to pour through their branches. Dane led across the
forest in silence as Clifton followed close behind, pushing away low
branches and climbing over decayed logs. After a while, the trees
thinned, and the forest floor rose in leaf-covered drifts. The soft lap
of a river ebbed and flowed in the distance.

"Keep pace, lad," the dwarf said. "We will soon rest."

The drifts grew to small hills, and the dwarf weaved across
Clifton close at his heels, as if the little man had a built-in GPS.
Realizing the lapping river grew louder, Clifton laughed. The dwarf
did have a GPS. He was following the river.

The forest ended at a deep gorge cut through the mountain. A flush rock wall sloped down into the powerful river flowing like a stampede beneath a single-pass rope bridge.

"No, way," Clifton said.

Dane turned. "What's the problem, lad?"

"There is no way I'm crossing that old, rotten excuse for a bridge."

"Suit yerself," Dane said, taking a step onto the swaggering bridge. It creaked while the small man passed briskly across. From the other side, he called, "Well? Are ya coming or not?"

What choice did he have? With a deep huff, he stepped onto the bridge, both hands clutching the fibers of the knotted handrail. The boards swayed beneath him. He took another step. The bridge swung. He froze.

"The faster ya move, the less it shakes." The man's voice was barely audible over the raging river that raced beneath Clifton like rush-hour traffic. "Besides," Dane continued, "the longer ya stand there, the greater yer chances the ropes will snap."

"You've got to be kidding me," Clifton said, through clenched teeth. And with a scream, he sprinted across the quivering boards until he leapt off the bridge to the safety of steady ground, doubled over, panting panicked breaths.

"Now, that wasn't so bad," Dane said.

Clifton lifted his he'd enough to see the dwarf's crooked, little smile. "You're enjoying this, aren't you?"

"I wouldn't say that," the dwarf laughed.

After hours of walking, the sun perched directly overhead. Dane guided to a dirt path that led away from the river, the gorge, the forest itself, into high rocky terrain. Tall mountains surrounded them as the path followed the curves of the chain. Grass clumps patched between the rocks. Bright sunshine warmed them with drifting clouds providing shade. Clifton hadn't walked this much since hiking as a Boy Scout. And at least then he had some trail mix and a Gatorade to keep him company. Dane led to a shade tree, with grasping boughs and a thin trunk.

"It's time to rest," he said, opening his sack. He handed Clifton a portion of bread and cheddar cheese.

Clifton ripped off a bite of bread, cramming too much into his mouth. He barely chewed, swallowed, then crammed in more. The sharp cheddar melted in his mouth.

"Here," Dane said, handing Clifton a leather bottle.

Clifton lifted the bottle to his lips. Water poured out over the edges and dripped off his chin.

"Slow down, there. Yer wasting all our drink."

Clifton wiped his mouth with his sleeve. "Sorry. I didn't realize how thirsty I was." He handed the bottle back to Dane. The dwarf stared at it, as if regretting the notion to share, and took a sip.

Clifton finished his snack and propped up against a tree with a burrow in the trunk resembling a yawning monster.

"That feels better," Dane said, leaning back and letting out a sigh. "Now, are ya ready to hear more about the arrow?"

Clifton stared over at him. "Yes."

Dane took two apples from his sack and handed one to Clifton. "It was carved by Wisdom herself in the beginning. One of the five she created. This one here's the last in known existence. Few have been chosen by one of these arrows, and they have each won great victories because of it. Whoever controls the arrow controls the land." He took a knife from his pocket and began to peel his apple in one long strip. "It attaches itself to its chosen possessor, sorta like an extension of the lucky soul it grabs ahold of and passes on protection and wisdom."

"Is that why it moves? And glows? Like it's alive or something?"

"In a way, yes."

Clifton took a bite of his apple. "So, what powers does it have?"

"Many. Its greatest being the ability to prolong life."

Clifton stopped mid-chew. "Are you telling me this arrow can let you live forever?"

"It can. But maybe not quite the way yer thinking. It's complicated, Clifton. Remember what I said about the cake?"

"All of this is complicated," Clifton said, taking another bite.

"Aye, boy." Dane bit into his fruit. Suddenly, his eyes widened.

"It's said to have killed a cockatrice once." He spit out bits of apple as he spoke.

Clifton squinted. "What's a cockatrice?"

"I forget, boy, how our paths are not the same. The cockatrice is a dragon with the head of a rooster. Has the ability to turn man into stone with a single look and is even said to have killed with breath alone."

"And this arrow has killed one before?"

"Perhaps not that arrow in particular, but one much like it, aye. By Sir Geoffrey of Regulus in the tenth century. He found the arrow in his possession, much in the same way you have. His village had been tormented by the beast; each warrior executed by the dragon's stare. Even roosters brought to crow—one of the only known ways to kill a cockatrice—were slain before their mouths could open." Dane chewed and continued talking without swallowing. "Sir Geoffrey took the arrow and laid aim while the cockatrice burned his village. Before the beast knew what hit him, the arrow landed in its heart, glowed white-hot, and disintegrated the dragon to ashes."

"Wicked," Clifton said.

"Aye, the beast was very wicked, indeed."

Clifton smiled at the misunderstanding.

"Sir Geoffrey later became king and ruled for two hundred years."

Clifton's brow furrowed. "I don't know, Dane. I find that hard to believe."

"Don't doubt the truth, lad." He leaned in close. Deep lines creased his forehead, and crow's feet bordered his eyes. "Do ya wonder how old I am?"

Clifton nodded.

"Well, I won't be telling you that. None of yer business."

"Then why'd you ask?" Clifton said, reaching for the leather bottle.

"You wouldn't believe me if I told ya."

"I'm having a hard time believing any of this." He took a swallow and handed the bottle back. "I keep telling myself it's a dream."

"Reality is not always defined by what ya know. It is best defined by what ya feel, here." He pointed toward Clifton's stomach. "Tell me, what does yer gut tell ya?"

"That I'm still hungry?" He grinned. Dane didn't.

"Do ya know what the arrow is made from?" Dane asked.

Clifton shrugged, his head resting on his knees. "Wood and feathers?"

"Not any wood and feathers. The wood is from the Tree of Knowledge and the feathers from the Simurgh. Have ya heard of her?"

Pulling up blades of grass, Clifton said, "Not in many of the children's stories I grew up with. But you are—"

"You foolish child!" Dane shouted. "You will never know yer purpose if ya won't take this seriously." Dane's blue eyes narrowed. "You have been given a great gift, boy."

Clifton felt about as big as the dwarf. "I'm sorry. I didn't mean to offend you."

"Yer the only one offended here."

"I know I don't seem to, but I really am trying to understand."

Dane took a few bites from his apple before continuing. "The Simurgh is the all-knowing bird of reason, who nested in the Tree of Knowledge and conversed with King Solomon. It is her feathers that fuel the arrow's magic."

"How?"

"There are curative powers in her feathers. That is where the ability to prolong life lies."

Clifton rested his head against the tree and closed his eyes. He wanted to cry. He wanted to run home. But he couldn't even figure out how to make himself wake up.

"Clifton, I know it's difficult."

Clifton opened his eyes, holding back tears.

"Just remember, yer gut will never lead ya astray." He clapped him on the back, then stood. "I think you've heard enough for now. We have more land to cross before we reach the village, and we must make haste. It's still not safe out in the open."

Clifton slid his arms into his straps. "You said last night that the king knows I'm here. What is that all about?"

"By title, Richard the third is the king of England, but not her true king. By the standards of many, he's a thieving brute whose only desire is power and gain. Stole the throne from his own nephews, the boys we're meeting in Flaxton."

"Does the king know about the arrow? That I—have it?"

"Yes, lad. I'm afraid he does." Pressing through the rocky land, they followed the sun as a compass.

Clifton shook his head. "But how could he?"

"How he came about such knowledge is of no importance. What matters is that he knows. And he will do all that he has to in order to take the arrow from ya."

"Woah, woah. What do you mean all that he has to? He's not gonna try to...*kill* me. Is he?"

"Let's hope he doesn't succeed. Now, no more talking until we reach the village."

A wave of nausea flushed through Clifton's body. His knees buckled. Was the king watching them right now, like the eyes in the forest? Clifton gulped hard, tentatively moving forward. He imagined the mountains ripe for hidden archers behind boulders and poised canons camouflaged with moss.

King Richard III? He had heard that name somewhere, recently, on the news, he thought. He tried remembering. And although he didn't follow politics, he was certain a queen ruled England and not a king. Hadn't it been that way for hundreds of years?

And then, he knew.

"Dane!" He rushed to the dwarf. "I have to know one more thing."

Dane huffed. "One more thing, then that is all until we reach Flaxton."

"What year is it?"

Dane twitched his nose. "I was afraid ya might ask."

"What are you talking about?"

Through pursed lips, Dane said, "Clifton, it's best if ya wait. We're already lagging behind the sun." He took a step down the path.

Clifton grabbed the dwarf by his shoulders, forcing him to stop and face him. "What year is it, Dane? Tell me. Now."

The dwarf lowered his head then brought up his eyes to meet Clifton's. "We are in the year of our Lord, fourteen hundred and eighty-five."

"1485? How is it even possible that I'm here?"

"I don't know, lad. I've been wondering the same thing."

Chapter Seven

Flaxton Village

F laxton Village was surrounded by a three-story granite block wall, the gate of which, swung wide open. A single watchman with greasy hair, a stubbly beard, and a large scar across his cheek allowed Dane through without a second glance. When Clifton passed, that guard thrust his pudgy finger into Clifton's chest.

"State your business."

"His business is his own," Dane said, back-stepping and pushing Clifton through the gate. "Unless you'd like to take it up with Jasper Tudor."

The watchman's eyes widened, then relaxed. He grunted, mumbling under his breath as he motioned them through.

"Not very tight security," Clifton said.

"Put yer hood up, boy," Dane instructed, lifting his own. "And keep yer head down."

Clifton covered his head, suddenly overcome with fear. Along the perimeter, log houses, securely cemented with mud-mortar, lined the city streets. Horse urine fouled the air. Women gathered at the central well to gossip, and Clifton shifted his covered head to eyeball them. He felt like he was in a movie like he had been written-in to *Robin Hood*. Except, in this place, everything was real.

They scuttled through the busy marketplace. A peasant woman with leathery skin and thinning hair hollered, "Fleece blankets, keep ya warm," and then another one, with two little girls clinging to her skirts, competed with the first yelling, "Candles, getcha candles."

"Fresh fruit, Sir?" asked a small boy with knobby features.

Clifton shook his head.

"Thread, spun cotton and wool," called a young girl, about fourteen-years-old, with dark hair pulled tight beneath a handkerchief.

Clifton caught her eye, and he felt his cheeks flush. He nearly knocked into a jester blowing a flame for a gathered crowd, jumping out of the way before his hair got singed.

"Oy!" the jester yelled, " Watch your step."

As they moved to the edge of the marketplace, a gnarly looking blacksmith, with burns covering his arms, wielded swords and shoed horses. Soldiers monitored the streets. Puppeteers with knights on strings jousted for a small crowd of wide-eyed children.

A group of men sat in the open drinking ale, and by the sounds of them, plenty of it. A young girl approached, carrying a pitcher and ladle, her eyes downcast. "Ale, Sirs? Just one copper?"

"I'll take more than that," said a man yanking her into his lap. He cackled, and Clifton could see that all of his teeth were on vacation.

"Please, let go, Sir," the girl said, dropping her pitcher as she squirmed to break free.

Clifton stopped. Why wasn't anyone doing anything? Where were the soldiers? He took a step toward her when Dane grabbed him by the cloak.

"What the blazes are ya doing?" he asked.

Clifton pointed. "Helping her."

"Leave that for the soldiers, lad. Yer in no place to draw attention to yerself."

A soldier grabbed the man by the scruff of his neck and lifted him out of the chair, which knocked the girl to the ground. "That's the fifth time today you've been told to leave her alone," the soldier said. "Can't bother her from inside a locked cell, which is where you;ll be until the Sheriff comes."

"Come on," the man shouted. "We's having some fun. Ain't we, cheeky?" His cackle rasped out, but quickly ceased as the soldier dragged the man kicking and screaming. The young girl lifted her empty pitcher and headed off the main street without a word. At least that man couldn't bother her anymore.

As they left the market district, Flaxton quieted. Attached quarters lined the streets, then an inn with a bar on the bottom floor and an outdoor stairwell that led to the rooms for rent above. The din of patrons wafted out to the street, then silenced, after they passed.

Dane finally stopped in front of a dilapidated building. He rapped his knuckles on the door twice, then pounded a heavy fist once. He smiled at Clifton.

"What, is that your secret knock?" Clifton asked.

"If I told ya that, then it wouldn't be a secret no more."

"You don't have to tell me. I heard it. Three raps and a pound. Easy."

Dane turned, opened his mouth, then closed it. "Just be quiet, lad."

Clifton studied the flimsy wooden structure. "Don't they condemn buildings in the Middle Ages?"

"Want an apple, dear?"

Clifton turned sharply, startled by an old hag who had appeared out of nowhere. She held an apple so close to Clifton's face that his eyes crossed.

"Stand down, woman," Dane barked, pushing her aside. "He doesn't carry any coin."

The woman glared, rebuking Clifton with a hand gesture he had only seen on tv and continued on to the next prospect.

After what felt like forever, the peephole door slid sideways. A pair of dark eyes, attached to a dark-skinned face, peered through the small square. The dark man looked down at Dane, then Clifton, then back at Dane before sliding the peephole closed and opening the heavy wooden door.

Scanning the area one last time, Dane said, "Get inside."

Clifton stepped into the entranceway, and Dane closed the door behind them. The foyer smelled damp and old. It was so dark, Clifton had to use his ears as his eyes, listening as Dane and the dark man shuffled up the hollow steps of the stairwell, until Clifton heard hinges creak.

From the top of the steps, a door opened, and light flooded the stairwell, silhouetting Dane's frame. Clifton groped for the railing, his eyes slowly adjusting as Dane moved to the side, and the light spilled across the stairs. When he reached the top step, the door closed with a thump and Clifton jumped. The dark man stood behind him.

"Clifton, this here's Jasper Tudor," Dane said.

Jasper nodded with a slight bow. "It is an honor, Sir Clifton."

He stood tall and thin, with long robes that hung over his lanky body, reminding Clifton of his bathrobe when his brother, Pierce, put it on. Only Clifton didn't think Jasper would 'grow into it.'

"Nice to meet you," Clifton said with a nod.

"Clifton, Jasper, and I need a minute. Why doncha take a seat over there by the wall and wait."

"Sure," Clifton said, walking to the wooden chair. Jasper turned, his robes dragging like a shadow, and led Dane out of the room.

Just before he left, Dane turned and said, "And don't be touching anything."

Clifton crossed his heart with his finger, putting on the best *I promise to be good* face he could muster. But as soon as he was alone, he jumped up and skirted about the long table sitting in the center of the L-shaped room.

Glass jars lined a shelf filled with red and blue liquids, gelatins with herbs, amphibian parts, and bugs. He thought he had stumbled upon a science lab. But, actually, being in Medieval England, this was probably a sorcerer's stash. One jar contained a small bulb, which looked like an eyeball. Clifton tapped the side of the glass, and the solution vibrated, but not like water would, more like hair gel.

At the window, he pulled the heavy drape aside and let bright sunlight seep in. He looked beyond Flaxton's walled borders to the rolling green hills of the countryside. A river intersected far in the distance, and he could barely tell the outline of a castle on a faraway mountain.

Suddenly, Clifton swore someone moved through a break in the leaf-covered branches below the window. He pressed his face against the glass, trying to focus beneath the tree's crown. He stared for several minutes but couldn't see anything out of the ordinary. *"You're being paranoid. Stop freaking out,"* he told himself, closing the drapes. But he couldn't shake the feeling that someone was watching him.

An immense floor-to-ceiling bookshelf covered the wall opposite the window; parchments packed the shelves beside books with spines detailed in velvet and gold. Clifton read the titles out loud. *"How to Win Wars. Solidifying Your Kingdom with Arranged Marriage. The Geography of Sylvania."* He rolled his eyes. "Boring." He kept looking, finding titles that sounded more appealing. *"Dragons, a Study of Origin and Etymology. Herbs and Funguses Which Heal. The Sword in the Stone: Arthur's Rise from Rags to Riches, a Biography.* No way." Clifton took down this last book and blew off dust. He coughed, fanning the air in front of him. Opening the book to a random page, he read.

...Arthur had been an ordinary boy and the idea that he could be instrumental in something amazing had never occurred to him.

"I had heard of the sword as a lad," Arthur said. *"But I never thought I would have something to do with the legend coming to pass. Even more astounding was the moment I realized that it was me of whom the legend spoke, and the sword in the stone had been fashioned for my hands to hold..."*

Clifton looked back at the cover and reread it. Wasn't *The Sword in the Stone* a myth? He replaced the book, shaking his head. "Where's Google when you need it?"

Beside the bookshelf sat a desk scattered with parchments.

Clifton flipped through the plans and maps and decrees scribed in thick, black pen. He lifted a quill feather and dipped it into the ink bottle near the edge of the desk and tried writing his name on one of the parchments. It took too long, and he didn't make it past the 'L', grateful he wouldn't have to do homework in the Middle Ages.

A detailed drawing of a dragon with a spiky hammer tail and thick claws caught his eye. The parchment, dated June 16th, 1484, accounted for Sir Edwin, the Lionheart of York, slaying a long-tailed crest back dragon.

Clifton's palms sweat as he studied the image of the crocodilian with a fleshy beard that hung beneath its snout. "Can shoot out fire up to ten yards?" he read. "I hope this is research for a fiction novel." But as he looked at the outstretched, bat-like wings, he had a feeling someone wrote this parchment for the history books. "If you *are* real, I hope you're extinct."

A door creaked. Clifton dropped the parchment and rushed back to his seat, pretending to look bored, like he'd been sitting there the whole time. Dane's face showed he wasn't buying it, but with the procession, led by Dane and Jasper Tudor, then the two boys Clifton assumed were the king's nephews, his disapproval would have to wait.

The first boy looked to be about fourteen with short, brown hair and a stocky build, while the younger one, maybe eleven, had green eyes and a blond, scraggly mop of hair on his head. They stopped in the middle of the room. Jasper stared at Clifton. Clifton squirmed. Dane cleared his throat, motioning for Clifton to stand, and he jumped to his feet, his face reddened with embarrassment.

"Clifton, may I present to you Edward V," Jasper said, "the rightful heir to the throne of England." The older boy nodded his head. "And his brother, Prince Richard Plantagenet." Mop Head smiled.

Jasper then turned to address the two princes. "Your Majesties, may I present Clifton Chase from the Park of Wickham."

"It's actually called Melbourne. Wickham Park is not really...Never mind."

Edward stepped forward and circled Clifton. "So, you are the boy who stole my property."

Clifton looked at him. "Excuse me?"

"My arrow. You stole it, and I want it back."

Clifton took a step back. "I don't know what you're talking about. I didn't steal anything."

Edward and his little brother shared a glance. "So, you do not have the arrow?" Richard asked.

They were tag-teaming him. What was going on? These were the boys that were supposed to help him. "I have an arrow that I found in my closet if that's what you mean."

"I see," Edward said.

He wished he could throw a folding chair at Richard or jump off the table with an elbow to Edward's mouth. He grew angrier as the princes sized him up.

Edward shook his nose up in the air. "Then you must be a spy."

"A spy? For who?" Clifton asked.

"For my uncle. Thieves hire thieves."

Clifton glared at him. "I'm not a thief. I already told you I didn't steal anything. According to the dwarf," he said, motioning accusatorially at Dane, "the arrow chose me. You wanna explain why *your* arrow picked *me*?"

"How dare you, you insolent boy. I do not like your implications. Or your tone."

"With all due respect, I don't like your tone, S-i-r-e." Clifton dragged out the word with disdain. "I didn't ask to come here. I didn't ask for this arrow. I don't even know how I got here. So maybe you could back off."

The boys stood inches from one another. This would not end pretty. Richard stepped in between them. "Now, now brother. He has returned your arrow, no harm done. In my estimation, no spy of uncle's would do such a thing, would he?"

Edward turned away and ambled to his seat at the table. Clifton swung his backpack across his back and imagined the prince falling back in his chair after Clifton clocked him a good one, square in the jaw.

Edward called Jasper Tudor to his side and whispered something in his ear. Jasper whispered back, and this went on for several minutes. Finally, Edward waved Jasper aside.

Addressing Clifton, he said, "I have decided that you are not a spy."

"Well, isn't that dandy," Clifton said.

"Clifton," Dane warned through clenched teeth. "Yer manners."

"Now that we have moved on from that point, it is time for you to show me my arrow," Edward said.

Clifton hung his thumbs from the straps on his pack. "How do I know it's your arrow? It was in my closet. Maybe it doesn't want to be in the hands of a...self-pronounced king."

"Clifton," Dane said. "Enough!"

Edward's face contorted. "How dare you insult me. Give me the arrow at once!"

"Come and get it," Clifton said, "Your Majesty." He bowed low, keeping his eyes fixed on Edward.

Dane pushed Clifton out of the way and bowed. "Sire, please forgive my friend here. He seems to have left his manners elsewhere." Dane held his hand out to Clifton, his blue eyes constricted. "The arrow, boy. Now!"

Clifton's mouth gaped open. "What? You're on his side?"

Dane pressed into Clifton's chest, pushing him down into his seat. "This is not about you, boy. You give up the arrow, or I'll take it from ya." Dane's chest heaved; his face strained.

Infuriated, Clifton threw his backpack to the ground. He pulled out the arrow, hiding his amazement as it grew to its regular size. "Take it," he said, forcing it into Dane's chest. He crossed his arms. "That arrow's been nothing but trouble for me." Clifton slouched in his seat, looking at the mason jars on the shelf.

Dane took the arrow with an exaggerated smile. "There, now. Was it worth all that fuss?"

Clifton ignored him.

"Yer Highness," Dane said as he approached Edward with a bow. He handed the arrow to the prince then backed away.

Clifton cast a glance at Edward as he snatched the arrow from Dane. A smile wormed across his face exposing crooked, yellow teeth. "Finally," Edward said. "The Arrow of Light."

The Simurgh feathers swayed in an invisible breeze. Clifton couldn't help but stare, skeptical that the shaft glowed in someone else's hands besides his own.

So, it had a name.

It was called the Arrow of Light.

Chapter Eight
Found

E dward's face softened with the arrow in his hand.

"Thank you," he said to Clifton. "My apologies for questioning your loyalty. You have proven where you stand."

Clifton shrugged.

"Please, join me at my table."

Dane nudged him in the arm. "Take a seat, boy."

Clifton tromped across the floor and yanked his chair out with a screech. He sat down heavily at the large table and crossed his arms, determined not to be nice even though the prince had apologized.

Big deal.

Jasper returned from another room with a tray of fresh fruit, cubed cheese, and a loaf of bread. He showed them to the prince, who nodded approvingly before Jasper set down the tray. Dane removed the dried meat he'd brought and passed it to the prince. Edward smelled it, and then took a small bite.

"Mm. What taste is this?" Edward asked.

"Pheasant," Dane said. "With dill. That's Liv's touch."

"Remarkable. Thank you."

Dane smiled, and Clifton rolled his eyes. Man, that dwarf sure was pleased with himself. Richard poured a golden drink into detailed iron goblets set on the table.

Edward lifted his. "A toast. In remembrance of my mother and father, let us drink to love, friendship, and bravery. May the will of God be done."

With another nudge from Dane, Clifton lifted his cup. Goblets struck around the table. He took a large swallow, then gasped, wishing he'd tried a sip first. It went down like liquid fire. "What is this stuff?"

"This drink," Richard enunciated, "is a honey liquor called mead. Have you never tried any before?"

"Ugh, no. It's terrible."

"Well, that is a first," Richard said, offended. "I have been given this recipe from the Monks in the Abbey of Merevale themselves. A rarity, I can assure you." He looked like he was about to cry.

"Oh, sorry," Clifton said. "I didn't realize." He sipped this time, and it didn't burn so much. He tried to recover. "It isn't bad. Is there fruit in it?"

"Yes," Richard said, no longer looking like he would cry. "Raisins and orange peels, a secret addition of the monks."

Clifton was starting to feel relaxed.

"Please, Clifton. Tell us of your adventures," Edward said, popping a grape into his mouth.

Clifton grabbed a slice of bread and took a bite. "Well, like I already told you, I found that arrow in my closet, and it brought me here."

"How?" Richard asked. "It's intriguing."

He had to admit he enjoyed the attention, and he finally loosened up. "I was at archery club, and I had a bet going to win a beautiful emerald-green cam bow. I had bet the arrow--"

"You wagered the arrow?" Edward asked, flabbergasted.

"Well, I didn't know what kind of arrow it was when I agreed to the bet," Clifton defended. "I thought it was one of my grandpa's old arrows. It looks like a piece of junk when it's not glowing."

"A piece of what?" Richard asked.

"You know, junky. It looks old."

"It is old," Dane said.

"What is this junky, you speak of?" Richard asked.

"I can't believe you placed a wager using the arrow," Edward added.

"Can I talk here?" Clifton asked. They quieted, staring at him. "Do you want me to finish my story?"

"Of course." Edward motioned for everyone to quiet. "Please, continue."

Clifton sipped his mead, finding that it tasted better with each sip. "So anyway, like I was saying. I had the arrow ready to shoot. I pulled back on the string, and BAM!" He slapped his hands together demonstratively. "It disappeared." Looking at Edward, he said, "That arrow really is a terrible shot, in case you don't know. Anyway, when I finally found it, I was here, in a field somewhere in England, in the year 1485. Far from my home and even farther from my own time."

"Amazing," Richard said. "Traveling through time. Does this often happen in the future?"

Clifton's eyebrow rose. "You don't find any of this strange?"

"Strange? Are you jesting? I find it fascinating."

Under his breath, Clifton said, "Sure, handling it better than I did."

"We have heard of stranger things."

"Really?"

"Of course," Edward continued. "Magic and mermaids and—"

"Mermaids," Richard said, his pupils widening. "My favorite."

"Mythical swords," Edward continued, "and arrows that bring a boy from a different time and place to our own. There are many extraordinary things that we have been made aware of."

"So, you've known I'm from the future, and you never thought twice about it?"

"The arrow chooses whom it chooses," Edward said. "For whatever reason, it decided yesterday to bring you here."

"That's when I went looking for him, Highness," Dane said. "I'd received word that the boy was lost in the forest and went out to retrieve him. But it seems that..." Dane paused.

"That, what, dwarf?" Edward said. "Continue, please."

Dane nodded. "Yes, Majesty. It seems that your uncle already knows that Clifton is here. And of what he carries."

Richard pounded his fists on the table, rocking the goblets. "How could he know such things? Who is spying for him?"

"Who is not spying for him, brother?" Edward said. "We must keep a watchful eye on everyone outside our circle. Even those who have proven their allegiance in the past must prove their allegiance again until our uncle is brought down from the throne."

"Can I ask you something?" Clifton said.

Edward nodded. "Of course, you may."

"I don't understand why your uncle is in power if the throne belongs to you. Why can't you just take it back?"

The princes' laughed.

"If it were that easy, it would already have been done," Edward said, taking a drink. "When my father died, God rest his soul, I became the king of England. I was twelve-years-old, and many insisted I was too young and inexperienced to rule in my father's place. I am sure they were correct in their decision. A royal council was formed to rule on my behalf until my coming of age. This infuriated my uncle, who felt his age and experience should precede my God-given right to the throne."

Clifton ate a piece of dried meat, the sinewy flesh ripping in his molars with a tug.

"Richard and I were sent to the Tower of London, like common prisoners, by our fiendish uncle. It was a disgrace. If Jasper and Dane had not rescued us, I am most certain we would have been left there to die. A simple act of strangulation or poison dripped into our food. It is easy to kill someone when no one else knows where they are."

Clifton forced the meat down his tightening throat, realizing no one knew where he was except those in this room and the king. Facing Edward, Clifton said, "So you were sold out by your own uncle?"

Edward huffed. "Not sold, Clifton. Locked up. I mean, really. Are you listening?"

Clifton grinned. "I forget. We have different words for different things back home."

"Well, please try to remember your place here."

"It's pretty hard, I mean, you have no idea what I've been through," Clifton said.

"What *you* have been through?" Edward said. "Have you ever lost your family and your home in one day?"

Clifton shrugged. "Sort of, I mean, I am stranded here. It's not like I hopped a plane and worm-holed to England on vacation."

The table quieted, each of them staring at Clifton. "Your speech is confusing," Edward said. "If you cannot be clear, then hold your tongue."

Clifton took in a breath to tell the prince how he really felt, when Dane stomped his toes with the solid heel of his boot. "I'm sure Clifton has no intention of disrespecting ya, Highness. Yer mercy in this situation is most appreciated."

Edward nodded. "You are right, dwarf. I am beginning to see how this situation could be construed from one in Clifton's position."

Dane stomped Clifton's foot again.

"Thank you, Your Highness," Clifton said, hoping that would prevent Dane from bashing his toes a third time.

Edward continued. "To prevent further complications, uncle had the church declare our parent's marriage illegal, renouncing my rights to the throne permanently."

"What does that mean?" Clifton asked.

Richard jumped to his feet. "If our parents were never married in the sight of God and law, then our mother was pregnant out of wedlock, and we were born illegitimately. He stole our birthright and our heritage!" Tears rolled down the reddened cheeks of the younger brother.

Clifton couldn't imagine losing his family or never being able to return home. He hoped that wasn't his fate. "I'm sorry," he said. "I had no idea."

The whirring came first, then the window shattered, sending shards of glass tearing through the heavy drapes and flying into the room. A soaring metal ball bounced off the far wall and settled in the center. It took him a moment to realize they were even under attack, and Clifton held his breath, hoping that exploding cannonballs hadn't been invented yet.

"He has found us," Edward said, standing so quickly he knocked his chair to the floor.

In a few seconds, as if time had slowed to a drip, Clifton viewed the room come to life. Jasper threw Richard over his shoulder and carried the prince out of the room. Dane grabbed his sack and strapped it across his back, hurrying to the side of the window. He jumped, barely avoiding another cannonball hurtled through the already crumbling glass.

"How many?" Edward asked while gathering his weapons and strapping his gear into place.

"Hard to say," Dane replied. "Perhaps a dozen or more."

"Clifton," Edward said. "You must take the Arrow of Light with you." He held the arrow out to Clifton.

"No, way," Clifton said, stepping back. "I've had enough of that thing. It's yours, remember?"

"You must take it," Edward said, as he shoved the glowing shaft toward Clifton's chest. "If my uncle gets this arrow in his hands, the entire kingdom will be in danger. It will remain safe with you in your world."

"But I'm just an ordinary boy," Clifton said. "This isn't my problem."

Edward stepped closer, his face no longer resembling a boy of Clifton's age, but for the first time, he looked like a king. "You are the one, Clifton. The arrow has chosen you."

Chapter Nine
Running

C lifton raced down the narrow stairwell and back to the foyer, wedging the arrow into his backpack. Light spilled in as he opened the heavy oak door, and he shielded his eyes with his forearm.

"Run, boy," Dane yelled, waving him on. "Don't stop 'til ya reach home!"

Reach home? How was he supposed to do that?

Clifton darted down the street, back to the bustling marketplace, weaving between girls carrying pitchers, and shoving through endless crowds. He shot a glance over his shoulder. Was someone chasing him? As he faced forward, he slammed into the rear end of a horse, which neighed and shimmied sideways, allowing Clifton to step in the piping hot pile of manure it had recently dumped in the street.

"Grosse," he said. To make matters worse, he saw he was right about being followed, as some guy with black hair was chasing him.

Clifton spun around and knocked into a juggler who dropped a flaming stick on his own foot. "You imbecile!" the juggler said, while Clifton tumbled past off-balanced. With muscles tensed, he ran double-time through the dusty main street from the unknown man.

Up ahead, a young girl crossed his path. Clifton bounced around her while the old hag he'd seen when he arrived stepped out from behind a fruit cart, right in front of him.

"Watch out!" Clifton shrieked.

The hag looked up in time to pull back as Clifton flew toward her. He missed her by a fraction of an inch, but slammed into the cart, spilling fruit across the main road.

"Buffoon!" the plump vendor shouted. "Watch where you're going!"

Clifton jumped up and looked back down the fruit-covered street, his stalker nowhere to be seen. The peddler continued to scream, a crowd gathered, and scraggily kids stole all the blackcurrant, oranges, and strawberries they could carry before being shooed away. With the city gate within sight, Clifton quickened his pace, plowing toward the opening like a boulder rolling downhill.

"Oh, no ya don't," bellowed the watchman, grabbing Clifton by the collar and jerking him back.

"Let me go!" Clifton said, struggling to break free. It was the watchman who gave him trouble when he had first entered Flaxton.

"There ain't no way I'm lettin' go of ya. Not with them soldiers making chase."

So that's who was following him.

"I'm warning you; you'd better let me go," Clifton said again.

The watchman laughed out a breath saturated with alcohol and tobacco. He shifted toward Clifton, so they were locked face to face. "And why is dat, exactly?"

Clifton smirked. "Because this is gonna hurt." Clifton pulled the watchman's hand to his opened mouth and, without a single ounce of regret, bit down as hard as he could.

The man screamed and released Clifton, recoiling his wounded hand. "Why, yer a...yer an animal!" He looked down at the impression of Clifton's teeth in his skin. "Can't believe ya bit me!"

Not allowing the watchman time to retaliate, Clifton kneed him in the groin before the man knew what hit him. He grabbed between his legs and, with a high-pitched squeal, went cross-eyed then collapsed to the ground where he writhed in a tight ball.

Leaning over him, Clifton gloated, "I told you to let go."

"Clifton, run!" Dane yelled from down the street.

In the distance, led by the man Clifton had spied following him, a small pack of manned horses galloped toward the gate. The king's soldiers. Clifton backed away; his eyes glued on the entourage coming straight for him.

He needed a horse.

Off to the side, behind the guard gate, a brown and white stallion pulled against the rope attached to the hitching post. Clifton ran over, released the rope, and climbed on top of the beam for leverage. Balancing against the horse's back, he threw one leg across and pushed his full weight onto the stallion.

"Go," he shouted. The horse didn't budge. "Run?" Still, nothing. What would the guard say, Clifton wondered, assuming it was his horse? Clifton kicked the stallion's sides and shouted in his best, gruff voice, "Move it, ya beast!" and the stallion barreled out the gate.

They charged through the field away from Flaxton Village, and Clifton didn't dare to stop or look back, hoping the others had made their escape. He galloped over familiar rocky terrain, past the lone tree, and through the sandy clumps of grass. Clifton's only thoughts were of home. The stallion's shoed hooves tore up the earth, forced to keep running without a break, while the forest beckoned a promising sanctuary within its dense leaves and layered branches.

From behind, the steady gallop of hooves hitting hard soil resounded, and Clifton stole a quick glance. The same four riders from the village. While his legs cramped from holding tight to the horse's body, a second wind pushed him onward. Tightening the reins, he commanded the stallion to run even faster until they reached the woods.

Clifton passed over pine needles and leaves, ducked under low-lying branches, and hurdled the horse over roots and stumps. He maneuvered the stallion down a small pass off the main pathway.

The horses' clomping hooves continued to grow louder while the shouting riders approached.

They were gaining.

With no idea how to get home, his only hope was escape, so Clifton kept moving. It had taken him almost a day to reach this place. He could never outrun the horses, no matter how hard he tried, and he doubted he'd ever find his way back to the field, the one that had materialized and somehow taken him from Wickham Park.

What was he supposed to do?

In the distance, the faint rush of the river hummed. That was it. The river. If he could reach it fast enough, he could cross the rickety bridge and cut the ropes. The men would have to search for another way across. By then, Clifton would be long gone, maybe back at the cottage in Griffon Forest.

Maybe somehow on his way home.

He hoped.

He couldn't see the gorge or the river yet, but the ebb and flow intensified with each stride. Then, the large flat wall of the mountain came into view. He pushed his horse to keep running. He might make it.

Nearing the top of the hill, he spied the aged bridge and galloped toward it. It looked flimsier than he remembered, swaying ominously, threatening to prevent his escape. The rapids rushed and swelled over the rock-covered riverbank, and he jumped off the horse, knowing the king's soldiers would too. At least on foot, he stood a chance of escape, maybe even of finding his way home.

"Thanks, boy," Clifton said, running his hand down the stallion's smooth, shiny muzzle. As if understanding, the horse whinnied, shook his head, and trotted away.

Clifton eyed the hilltop as the men closed in fast. With a deep breath, he jogged across the bridge, his weight throwing the planks and ropes into a teeter. He made it halfway across when his footing slipped, and he shot out under the handrail, tumbling feet-first toward the rocks below. He managed to twist himself midair and catch the edge of a splintered plank, where he hung, clutching the boards, listening to the horses and riders reach the ledge.

The bridge tilted back and forth, certainly trying to throw him into the deadly rapids, mercilessly churning over the sharp rocks. The king's uniformed soldiers dismounted, with swords drawn, and two crossed the bridge. Clifton looked down. His grip on the mist-covered plank was slipping. The added weight of the grown men scuttling across the bridge sent it swaying farther out of control, and Clifton's fingers grew tired.

"Please, God," he prayed as his fingers failed to hold his weight and released the plank.

Flailing his limbs on the hundred-foot drop, Clifton fell heavy, slicing through the hungry river. He plunged deeper and deeper into blackness; the pressure unbearable. Finally, his body slowed and floated back toward the surface, and he kicked hard until he broke through the water's skin.

Clifton inhaled greedily, wading in the now still waters. The rocks and bridge had disappeared, along with the horses and their riders. Swimming in long strokes to the river's edge, he couldn't be happier that the current had brought him far away from danger and the rocks hadn't killed him in the process.

After several minutes of rest on the sandy shore, he pushed to his feet and looked around. Everything seemed wrong. Even if he had traveled far downstream, there would still be remnants of the river's banks and gliding water. But he saw none of that, no riverbank, no rushing water, no current whatsoever. He was staring at a lake — no doubt about it.

Exhausted, he moved up the hill away from the water and into the nearby trees grateful he hadn't lost his backpack during the fall. At least he still had the arrow. A sandy path formed, and Clifton took it, hoping it would eventually lead him back to the dwarves' cottage—assuming he had drifted back to that part of Griffon Forrest. Abruptly, the trees opened to a large field. Bright orange construction cones marked off a rectangular patch where kids waited in lines.

"There he is!"

Clifton looked up and saw Ava and Justin running toward him.

Somehow, he had made his way back to Wickham Park.

Chapter Ten
Out

"Clifton, where have you been?" Ava said, meeting him near the edge of the field.

"What are you guys doing here?" Clifton asked, not even sure where *here* was.

"Practicing," Justin said. "Why are you all wet?"

He wore his normal clothes again, not the strapped-on pants and frilly shirt he was wearing when he fell into the river. Boy, was he glad. On the one hand, he avoided utter embarrassment. On the other, he realized it *had* all been a dream. "I fell into the river."

"You mean the lake?" Justin corrected.

"Yeah, of course, I mean the lake."

"You don't look so hot," Ava said.

"I don't feel so hot." Clifton paced to a picnic table and plopped down on the bench. He leaned forward, his head resting between his legs, and stared at the ants crawling in the dirt.

"How'd you fall in?" Ava asked.

Clifton shrugged. How had he fallen in? He could feel Ava and Justin staring at him, waiting for an answer like he was some lab experiment gone wrong.

"What's today?" he asked, looking up.

"It's Friday," Justin said. "Are you okay?"

"It can't be Friday," Clifton mumbled. "I've been gone for days."

"What are you talking about," Justin asked.

"Or maybe, I never left," Clifton ranted, oblivious to his gawking friends. He checked his head for bumps to confirm his concussion suspicion but couldn't find any. "Maybe it was real. But how?"

"Maybe what was real?" Ava asked.

"Been gone where for days?" Justin said.

"Nothing. I... it's... I felt like I'd been gone for a long time, and... you know, figured maybe it wasn't real or something." His lips lifted to show the worst fake smile he had ever tried pulling off.

His friends weren't buying it. They eyeballed him like he needed a straitjacket. Wringing out the corner of his T-shirt, Clifton watched the water slosh to the ground over his muddy sneakers.

"I'm going to find your mom," Ava said, her voice rising with concern.

Before Clifton could protest, she turned to jog away. Great. There went his chances of ever getting Ava to look at him as anything more than friends. Not that he cared. Not really, anyway. Who was he kidding? Those flutters in his stomach, whenever she came around, could no longer be blamed on indigestion. No one had that much gas. Were things just simpler in elementary school?

Clifton knew the answer to his own question when Ryan walked over. "Well, look who decided to show."

Clifton wanted to smack the smile off his face. Ava must have known, too, because she never did leave to find his mom.

"Thought you'd run off with my arrow," Ryan said smugly.

"Wouldn't dream of it. Honestly, can't wait to get rid of the dumb thing."

"What were you doing near the lake?" Ryan asked.

"That's none of your business."

"You walk into The Hinterland over there, then show up over here near the lake a half-hour later, and no one saw you cross the field. Maybe I want to know what kind of freak you are so that I can protect myself."

Thirty minutes? Had it only been thirty minutes?

"How'd you pull it off with no one noticing?"

Clifton's scratched his jaw. "Well, I couldn't find the arrow at first. It shot way out in the dunes, as you said. Horrible precision. I think it's bent or something." He paused, looked at Ryan, hoping to lose his interest, which he didn't. "Anyway, I finally found it in a huge pile of dog crap."

"Gross!" Ava said.

"I don't know how you guys missed me. I walked across the field when everyone was lined up. Wanted to wash the arrow, squeaky clean, before I gave it to you, Ryan."

"Very thoughtful," Ryan said. "Let me have it."

"Sure, you want it?" Clifton asked. "Not easy to get poop off stuff without soap." He hoped Ryan would buy his story and lose interest in the Arrow of Light. He still needed to do some research on it. "And," he continued, "it's a terrible shot. Flies like it's motor-propelled. No way to control it."

"I'll take my chances," Ryan said. "Give it to me." He held out his open palm.

Clifton unstrapped his backpack and set it on the bench. "Okay. Whatever you say. But I'd recommend a serious washing when you get it home. Who knows what kind of worms and bacteria are still in the wood, bugs that lay eggs inside your intestines and--"

"Clifton, stop," Ava said. "That's disgusting."

Clifton unzipped his backpack and looked inside. "It's not here."

"What are you talking about?" Ryan asked.

"It's missing." He dug around, searching behind his sweatshirt and loose papers, knowing there was nowhere it could hide.

"Isn't that convenient," Ryan said. "I bet you hid it somewhere. That's why you were really at the lake."

"You calling me a liar?"

"If the shoe fits," Ryan said.

Clifton stood. "It was in my backpack."

"So you say," Ryan said, stepping close. "But I think you're a sore loser."

Clifton inched closer. "And I think you're just a loser."

Ryan cocked back his fisted hand, and Clifton blocked his face.

"Hold it guys," Justin said, his arms outstretched between them. He stared at Clifton. "What's the matter with you?"

"Me? You can't be serious!"

"Clifton, calm down," Ava said, her hands slowly lowering. "Please." Her green eyes pleaded with him to stop.

What was happening? Had everyone gone crazy?

"I'm out of here." He pushed past Justin, grabbed his backpack off the bench, and stormed off.

"You're a liar and a coward," Ryan called after him.

Clifton didn't respond. Not with the look Ava had given. Why did she all of a sudden think he was the bad guy? Couldn't she see Ryan was the one messing with him?

Clifton had only seen the kid a handful of times at school. Ryan never talked much unless he was picking on someone. Now he seemed to be targeting Clifton. How had that happened?

"Clifton, wait up."

He swiveled his head. Justin jogged up from behind. "What do you want?"

"Where are you going?" Justin asked.

"Home."

"Clifton, stop." Justin grabbed him by the shoulder. "What's up with you?"

The two boys stood alone in the middle of the field, the archery range at one end, and parked cars at the other. He leaned in close to Justin. "Something happened to me."

Justin lowered his voice. "What are you talking about?"

Clifton looked around. "We shouldn't talk in the open. Someone could be listening."

"Like who?"

Clifton guided to the trees surrounding the field. For some reason, he felt guarded beneath the leaves and limbs. "Okay. I know this is going to sound crazy, but that arrow I found in my closet, the one I bet against Ryan for his beautiful cam bow…"

"Yeah," Justin said impatiently. "What about it?"

"I think it's magic."

Justin's eyes squinted as he leaned back. "You joking with me, Chase?"

"Dude," Clifton said. "Does this sound like my normal kind of joke? Do you see me laughing?"

"No. But you gotta hear yourself, man. You sound loco."

"You're my best friend, J. I should be able to tell you anything."

"You can. I'm listening."

"I don't know how to explain it." Clifton shifted his weight, let out a deep breath. "I was looking for the arrow, that part was true, walking everywhere in The Hinterland. I never thought I'd find it. And then, it was there, sticking out of the ground. But when I touched it, when I picked it up—I wasn't here anymore. I wasn't in Wickham Park."

"What do you mean? Where were you?"

Clifton rubbed the back of his neck and shuffled his feet in the sand. "Forget it," he said.

"No way," Justin said. "You can't do that. You can't say something like that and then stop talking." He put his hands on Clifton's shoulders. "Bro, I'm your best friend. You can tell me anything. What happened to you?"

"You're just gonna laugh at me."

"Clifton, I swear to God, I won't laugh at you."

Clifton looked up. "You promise?"

Justin crossed his heart with his index finger and then raked it across his throat. "Hope to die," he said.

Clifton nodded. "I think I traveled through time."

Justin lifted a single eyebrow. "You what?"

"I think I time-traveled. It's like, one minute, I was in the dunes, and the next, I was in a field somewhere surrounded by mountains."

Justin held out his hand. "Hold on a sec," he said. "Are you trying to tell me that the arrow is like a portkey?"

"I don't know. I think it is. Or was. It's missing now."

Justin covered his mouth and looked away before his body shook, and he broke into a fit of laughter. "I'm sorry, man," he said, in hysterics.

Clifton pinched his mouth closed. "Thanks a lot."

"I'm sorry!" Justin yelled as Clifton stomped off to his mom's CRV and slammed the door closed.

He couldn't believe Justin. "Some friend." He laid his chair all the way back to peer out the sunroof at the dark clouds rolling in. Thank God he never told him about meeting a dwarf couple and some princes who'd been dead for a few hundred years.

But no matter how ridiculous it seemed, no matter how hard he tried convincing himself that Justin's reaction was justified, Clifton knew he'd traveled back in time, to the year 1485, where he met two princes, a dwarf and his wife, and a man named Jasper Tudor. And in his gut, like an idea about to take shape, the truth bubbled. The arrow really held the powers Dane suggested and Prince Edward had trusted Clifton to keep it safe and secure.

And he had managed to lose it.

Chapter Eleven

The Painting

C lifton showered and changed into clean clothes, racing the storm threatening to burst into a downpour. He sat at his desk. "It's time to get some answers."

According to the web, after the death of King Edward IV in 1483, his brother, Richard III forced his way into the throne by banishing his nephews, twelve-year-old Edward V and his younger brother Richard, to the Tower of London.

"That would have made Edward fourteen in 1485."

There was a knock at his door, and it opened. Clifton minimized the screen and swiveled around in his desk chair.

"Clifton," his mom said. "I want you off the computer. The storm is bad, and I don't want anything to short out."

"Okay, Mom. Just a minute."

"Now, Clifton," she said, closing the door.

Clifton swiveled back around to face the screen. He continued reading how a hefty bribe from King Richard III to the cardinal annulled Edward IV's marriage to Elizabeth Woodville, the princes' mother. Being unwed when she gave birth, according to the church and state, the princes' claim to the throne became null and void, leaving it to the next of kin: their uncle, Richard.

"What a snake," Clifton said. He read aloud. "Once in the Tower of London, the princes were never seen in public again." Clifton looked away from the screen. "That's not right. Jasper and Dane rescued them from the Tower of London. Unless..." He rubbed his temples. "Unless none of this really happened."

Clifton stared at the faces of Richard and Edward V on his computer screen. Although they were paintings, the resemblance to the boys in Flaxton Village was unmistakable. He knew it couldn't be just a coincidence. "No. Something else must have happened to them."

He stood and paced his room. "This is serious. I mean, what if they were supposed to be forgotten? What if they were supposed to die?" He stopped short, shaking his head. "No, no. That's not right." He began pacing again, running his fingers across the spines of his books. "Why would I be involved if they were supposed to die?" A chill cut up his spine, making him shake. "What if I'm supposed to change history?"

He moved back to his desk, yanked his chair back, and continued to surf. All the websites painted Richard III as a very bad king. It seemed his determination to protect his position meant cutting down any and every person with the slightest bit of power who could stand in his way. In 2013, Richard's skull was found under a parking lot in England. Clifton wondered if the skull contained any holes from a magical arrow.

"No, way," Clifton said, staring at the face of the dark man from Flaxton Village on his monitor. "That's Jasper Tudor." He read how King Richard banished him, too, for remaining a Loyalist to the throne of Edward IV, revoking Jasper's land and all his possessions. "That explains why he waited on the princes hand and foot."

He leaned back, his head throbbing. It was too much to handle. How could this even be happening? He knew there was no way he could have made up all those details in a dream, especially not with such accuracy. The explanation stared right at him. The information was as clear as a bell.

"This makes no sense," he moaned, dropping his head on his desk.

The wind beat heavy on his window, his room the same shade as the darkened, overcast sky. Clifton lifted his head.

Could he have really traveled back in time? To Medieval England? But why? He lit a candle, the low lighting reminding him of the dwarves' cottage. He hoped Dane made it home all right. He hoped the princes had escaped. He wondered if he'd ever find out because, as history was written, it wasn't a happy ending.

"Clifton," his mother called from outside his room. "Are you off the computer yet?"

"Almost, Mom," he shouted back.

Clifton read faster, about the conflict between the family and the War of the Roses, stopping short when he read about a girl nearly twenty years old named Lady Elizabeth Tudor. "The princes' sister? What did she have to do with any of this, and why hadn't anyone mentioned her?"

Clifton printed and printed documents until his eyelids screamed for a break. He slumped back in his seat. Thunder chased the approaching lightning, the boom shaking the house as the heart of the storm grew nearer.

He clicked on another link. This one showed a thumbnail of an oil painting depicting a great battle scene. Mounds of men and horses lay dead and wounded on a battlefield. Several soldiers clashed swords and axes; their mouths opened in many battle cries. A boy stood in the midst of them. He held an arrow in one hand and a bow in the other.

Clifton pushed his nose almost to the screen.

"What in the world?" he said.

He needed a closer look at the image, so he opened the page in an editing program. Lightning flashed closer; the rumbling thunder clapped louder.

"Clifton, now!" his mother yelled.

"Okay!" he yelled back.

The enlarged frame showed only pieces at a time of the painting, and he ran the cursor along the document searching for the boy's face, like swiveling a telescope's lens in space searching for a certain star. With the storm growing worse, he hit print, and the printer rumbled out the page slower than he liked.

Clifton jumped as a lightning bolt struck so close; he could have tasted ozone while thunder cracked. His computer "popped" then abruptly shut off. The black sky opened, dropping fat rain to the ground. "A transformer must've blown."

His mother poked her head in the dark room, the candlelight casting shadows on the wall. "I hope you got off before that lightning hit."

"I'm off, Mom," he said.

"Glad to see you have a candle burning. It may be a while before the storm lets up enough for the power company to fix whatever got hit."

He nodded. His mom closed the door. He checked his printer. Only half of the image printed before the power cut out. But it was enough to make the hairs on the back of his neck stand on end. He stared at the paper in his hands.

But it wasn't possible.

There was no explaining it, but here it was, the most substantiated proof that the trip to England really took place. He was sure in his gut, where Dane reminded him he would always find the truth, that he was the boy in the oil painting. And in the darkness, a glow suddenly streamed from his unzipped backpack. Clifton crossed the room and looked inside in amazement; his face reflected the light.

The Arrow of Light had returned.

Chapter Twelve

Revealing

C lifton stretched in the gymnasium at DeLaura Middle School. Over the weekend, he tried convincing himself that the trip to England never happened, and the strange glowing arrow, now hidden beneath his winter coat in the back of his closet, was a figment of his imagination. The two princes and King Richard III were figures in history. Nothing more. But the oil painting haunted him, the boy who looked too much like him in the middle of the battlefield carrying a bow and glowing arrow.

Coach Alonso blew his whistle and jogged out to the center of the basketball court, carrying a mesh bag of red rubber balls slung over his shoulder like a rejected Santa Claus. "Line up," Coach said. "Time for some dodgeball."

Moans and groans erupted from some of the girls while the students gathered on the white line.

"Count off in twos. One's to this side," Coach said, pointing to the left sideline. "Two's over there." He motioned for the twos to stand on the opposite side.

Clifton tried to subtly space himself out so he and Ava would be on the same side.

"Clifton," Coach said.

"Yeah, coach?"

"Get back to where you were."

"But I didn't—"

"Clif-ton," Coach said, with raised eyebrows.

"Okay, fine." Clifton hunched forward and stepped back in line.

"Two," said Justin, walking off to the north side of the gym.

"One," said Ava.

One. Please be a one. Please be a one...

But after a few more runs, Clifton forced himself to call out, "Two," and treaded over to his team. At least he would be with Justin.

With a light jab, Justin said, "Look who got a transfer to sixth period PE."

Clifton looked across the gym. Ryan Rivales flashed a huge white smile to Coach Alonso, his blond hair slicked and starched like the plastic head of a Ken doll. Coach motioned for him to join the south side's team, where he immediately made conversation with Ava. Clifton glared at Ryan, who turned and waved at him.

"Can you believe that guy?" Clifton asked Justin.

"What do you mean?"

"Look at him flirting with Ava like that."

Justin shook his head. "You're right, Clifton. What kind of kid on his first day of class tries to hit on the prettiest girl on the planet?"

"You're not very funny."

"Sorry, dude. I know he seems sort of like a scuzzball."

"Sort of?"

"Okay, so he's a scuzzball. But you did make a bet with him and then bail. That's pretty uncool."

"I told you, I lost that arrow," Clifton said. As far as he was concerned, Justin was on a strictly 'need to know' basis, best friend or not, after his reaction in Wickham Park.

"You weren't so bright to take that bet in the first place."

Clifton cocked his head in Justin's direction. "You said I had nothing to lose."

Who was this guy? It was like Justin's body had been taken over by aliens or evil pod people.

"That was me being supportive. You had your mind made up before I said anything."

"Whatever," Clifton said, his focus back on Ryan, who seemed oblivious to anyone but Ava. She giggled and smiled like she was engaged in the greatest conversation she had ever had in her entire life. Clifton frowned. "You don't think she likes that jerk, do you?"

"He's decent looking, built like an ox, probably the best athlete out here."

Yup, definitely pod people.

"Whose friend are you, anyway?"

"Look, Clifton. If you like the girl, why don't you ask her out?"

"Who says I like her?"

"Come on," Justin said, grinning. "Everybody knows you have a thing for Ava."

Clifton's ears went warm. "They do?"

"Yeah, and if everyone knows, then it's no secret to Ava. Hot gossip travels fast in this school. So, if you like her, ask her out. If you're too chicken, stop worrying about who she's talking with. It's getting old." Justin lined up in the front row.

"I'm not chicken," Clifton said, stepping in the back row near the edge of the court.

Coach Alonso blew his whistle for quiet. "The rules are simple. Throw the balls at opposing players while dodging their shots. No hitting a player who is already out, and no strikes to the head or below the belt. On my whistle."

Clifton kept his eyes on Ryan, who lined up in the front row facing Justin. His legs in a runner's stance, Clifton rubbed the sweat from his palms on his gym shorts. The whistle blew. Kids in the front lines shot forward, grabbing balls from the floor, then hurtled them across the gym. Clifton stayed light on his feet, bobbing and weaving as red balls whirred past. With a slight rotation at his hips, he barely missed a ball skimming by, but as he straightened, another one slammed into his chest with a thud.

"Out," Coach Alonso shouted.

Clifton jogged to the sidelines. From his peripheral, a red blur whizzed toward him. He turned, catching the full force of the ball square in the face before hitting the ground hard.

Coach Alonso blew his whistle. "No face shots."

Clifton checked his nose. It wasn't bleeding. His watering eyes felt like they'd been pushed back into his skull, leaving hollow sockets behind. Even though he could barely see, he knew exactly who had thrown that ball.

Coach Alonso knelt beside him. "You all right?"

Clifton pushed to his feet. "I'm fine."

"Do you need to go to the clinic?"

Clifton shook his head.

"I'll go grab an icepack from my office." Coach Alonso crossed the court toward his office in the back.

Searching the gym, Clifton found Ryan on the sidelines wearing a guilty smirk.

Clifton sprung toward him. "You threw that at me on purpose," he said.

"I'm sorry," Ryan taunted. "Were you already out?" His voice came out saturated in sarcasm like syrup on all-you-can-eat pancakes.

"You know I was already out."

"I know you suck at archery; now I know you suck at dodgeball, too."

Clifton advanced. "Is that what this is about? That stupid arrow?" He shoved Ryan hard in the chest.

Ryan shoved him back. "I couldn't care less about your busted-up arrow."

A couple of kids crowded around, as the two wrestled, egging on the reaction of rubberneckers. Coach Alonso did a one-eighty. He grabbed Clifton by the shoulders and pulled him off. "All right, that's enough. Cool it!"

"He knew I was out," Clifton said, still under the coach's tight grip. "He hit me on purpose."

"You walked right into it, you wimp," Ryan said.

"I said that's enough," Coach Alonso told Ryan. "Go have a seat."

Ryan strolled off the court, lifting his hands in an attempt to show surrender. Ava met him at the bleachers, sitting awfully close. Clifton's face burned from the blow. He imagined Ryan telling her his fabricated side of the story including, Clifton presumed, about his innocence.

Ava looked up from her conversation with Ryan. She was giving Clifton the same look his mom gave his dad when he messed up. Could she really be taking his side?

"He's lying!" Clifton shouted.

"You're coming with me," Coach Alonso said, dragging Clifton to his office and slamming the door behind them.

Clifton flopped down in a pea-green vinyl chair, his arms crossed. Coach Alonso opened the door to a miniature refrigerator near his desk. "Here," he said, tossing an icepack to Clifton.

Clifton placed the icepack on his throbbing cheek. It stung but soon numbed the pain. At least the pain in his face.

"Clifton," Coach Alonso said. "I must say, I'm disappointed in you. I expect you and every other student to treat each other with respect."

"But he threw the ball at me on purpose!"

"He did no such thing."

Clifton stared down at the concrete floor. What was the point in arguing?

"What got into you?"

"Coach, he doesn't like me."

"Are you sure it's not the other way around?" Coach Alonso asked, sitting behind his desk. "It looked to me like you were the one doing the pushing."

"What? Have you gotten a good look at my face?"

"Accidents happen."

"Accident? This was no accident. I can't believe you're taking his side too."

Coach Alonso took out a small notepad and began writing. "It's not about taking sides. It's about treating people fairly. I'm going to have to call your mother and tell her that you were fighting in class. I really hate to do this, Clifton. You're one of my star students."

"It wasn't fighting, Coach. It was self-defense."

"That's not how it looked to me. You'll have to take this note to the principal's office and wait for your mother to come pick you up." Coach Alonso moved to his office door and opened it. Holding the disciplinary note in his hand, he waited for Clifton to follow.

"What about him?"

"He doesn't concern you," Coach answered.

"This is so unfair!" Clifton said, throwing the icepack on the desk, avoiding the note like the plague.

"I'll be sure to include your tantrum in my report. You can take this up with your folks later."

Clifton stood and stomped toward Coach Alonso, grabbing for the note in his hand. "This is lame."

Coach put his hand out to stop Clifton. "You need to change your attitude, or you'll find yourself in detention, or worse."

Still clutching the note, Clifton asked, "Can I go now?"

After he felt the point had been made, Coach Alonso released the note.

Clifton pushed open the double doors that led to the gymnasium and rushed in. The doors boomed closed behind him, echoing off the walls and high ceiling. Everyone turned to stare. Clifton plowed across the sleek floor, his screeching sneakers the only sound, as every eye in the gym watched him pass. It felt like the gym stretched for miles. He hoped the far doors weren't just a mirage.

"See you later, buddy," Ryan hollered.

Clifton didn't look up, speed-walking across the polished floor. Reaching the far doors, he thanked God they were real and pushed one. Of course, it was locked.

"What a tool," Ryan said as the students erupted in laughter.

Clifton quickly pushed open the other door, glancing over his shoulder as he left. He caught Ava staring at him.

At least she wasn't laughing.

Chapter Thirteen

Grounded

C lifton slouched on the couch with his arms crossed. His dad, who usually traveled during the week for meetings, paced the living room rug, loosening his tie. Clifton couldn't remember the last time his dad had made it home this early. Of all the days to get in trouble at school.

His dad stopped pacing. "Do you have any idea how furious I am?"

Clifton wanted to say, *Yes, Dad. Of course, I do. I can see your blood pressure rising in that throbbing vein in your neck.* But he had learned from Mrs. Seaton's English class that this was a rhetorical question.

"Haven't I taught you that we don't solve our problems by fighting?"

"I wasn't fighting, Dad. I've told you already. It was self-defense."

Clifton's dad had now completely removed his tie. "Unprovoked attack is not self-defense."

"It wasn't unprovoked! He threw a ball at my face and knocked me to the ground on purpose."

"And you know that for a fact? You know what he was thinking?"

"You're not listening."

"Then talk to me. Why would this kid hit you on purpose?"

"The guy's a loser. He was probably trying to show off in front of Ava and—"

"Who?" his dad asked.

"Ava Harrington," Clifton's mom said from the kitchen. "She's very pretty."

"Okay, Mom," Clifton said. "We get it."

"Ohhhh," his dad said. "Now, I understand."

Clifton looked up at his dad. "What's that supposed to mean?"

His parents exchanged a glance.

"Coach Alonso said it was this boy's first day in your PE class," his dad explained. "It doesn't make any sense why he would attack you. But it does make sense that you would feel threatened if you saw him with Ava and…"

Clifton finally snapped. "It had nothing to do with her. God, why does everyone keep saying that?"

"Attitude check," his dad said. "Watch your volume."

"Watch yours," Clifton mumbled

"Clifton!" his mom said. "Don't talk to your father like that!"

"You better watch it," his dad said. "I'm losing patience with you."

"Yes, sir," Clifton replied.

Clifton's mom slipped into the living room and stood beside her husband. "Your father is *trying* to tell you that we're both disappointed with how you handled yourself. Isn't that right, Charles?"

Clifton stared at him, knowing he shouldn't be talking to his dad this way. If only he could tell the truth. Then his parents would understand what was happening. But that could never work. He'd have to explain a whole lot more than why Ryan was mad at him.

And that story could get him locked up for a long time in a place with padded walls.

"Your mom's right. We expect more from you. You need to make things right."

"How am I supposed to do that? Throw a ball at *his* face when *he's* not looking?"

"I want you to write an apology letter to Coach Alonso."

"I have to apologize to Coach? You're kidding, right?"

"You will apologize for your behavior today, young man."

Clifton nodded, defeated, playing with a frayed string on the bottom of his shirt. "Yes, Sir."

"And," his dad said. "I want you to write an apology letter to the boy you fought with."

"What!" Clifton said. "No, way. I'm not apologizing to that creep!"

"Yes, you are. And you can stay in your room until you finish both letters."

"This is so unfair!"

Clifton's mom retreated back to the kitchen. His dad's face turned tomato red and the vein in his neck, which had subsided, began twitching again. "You wanna talk about unfair? I finally have a day where I can come home early, to spend some time with my family and relax, and I have to deal with this?"

"Well, I'm sorry to have ruined your plans," Clifton said, pushing off the couch and down the hall. "I'll just spend the rest of my life in my room!"

Chapter Fourteen
Startled

C lifton slammed his bedroom door. Had he just grounded himself? This Ryan kid was messing up everything, flirting with Ava, turning his friends on him, and now his dad was mad. To top it all off, he needed to write an apology letter to the very person responsible for all of his problems. Unbelievable!

He sat at his desk and lit a candle, finding he liked it better than his lamp. Opening a blank Word document, Clifton typed:

Dear Ryan,

My dad wants me to write you an apology letter, so here it goes: I'm sorry that you are such a loser. Please stay away from me and my friends until you are no longer a moron.

In all insincerity,

Clifton Chase

Clifton balanced on the two back legs of his chair and reread the letter. *Not too bad*, he thought, his mouth curling in a smirk.

"Hello, lad."

The chair fell out from under him as Clifton lost his balance at the sound of the dwarf's voice. Reaching for his desk, he toppled books and knocked over his pencil holder, sending pencils flying across the tile floor. "Dane!" He sprung to his knees, grabbed the dwarf, and held him in a tight bear hug.

"Happy to see ya, too," Dane said.

Clifton let go and stood. "I can't believe you're here. I thought I'd made you up."

"Figure if ya were making things up, you'd have made me a bit better lookin' and with a more pleasant demeanor." He smiled. "Course, I'm real. What'daya think I was, a leprechaun?"

"How'd you get here?"

Dane shook his head. "Don't ask."

There was a knock at the bedroom door. "Clifton?" his mom said through the wood. "Are you okay?"

"Fine, mom," Clifton called back. "I fell." Grabbing Dane, he pushed him into the closet. "You've got to hide. The last thing I need is my mom seeing me talking to a dwarf." *Or worse. To no one at all.*

"Okay, I'm hiding," Dane said. "Stop shoving!"

"Be quiet." Clifton closed the closet door and crossed to his desk chair, picking it up as his mom walked in. "Hey, mom. What's up?"

"What happened here?" she asked, carrying in a plate of meatloaf, mashed potatoes, and string beans.

"I was balancing on the back legs of my chair like you always tell me not to, and I fell."

Shaking her head, she set his plate on the bedside table. "How are those letters coming along?"

Clifton quickly minimized the screen on his computer. "Okay. Still working on them." *While a dwarf from the Middle Ages hides in my closet.*

"Well, your dad and I agree that you'll have to have dinner in here tonight. But you may come out once you've finished those letters." She picked up his sneakers and reached for the closet doorknob.

"Wait!" Clifton yelled, sprinting over before she could open it all the way.

"What's wrong, Clifton? You scared me."

With her back to the opened door, she couldn't see what Clifton could, a light glowing from within the dark closet or Dane's silhouette, which stood clearly visible in the center. Clifton took the sneakers from his mother and scooted her away from his closet with his free hand. "Mom, I've got this. You work hard enough." He threw his sneakers in the closet, which might have struck Dane, and closed the door. "I'll clean this mess up as soon as I've finished with those letters. Promise."

His mom smiled. "That's great, buddy. Now eat your dinner before it gets cold."

"Okay, Mom," Clifton said, ushering her out of the room and closing the door. "All clear," he called to Dane.

Dane stepped out of the closet, wearing a scowl on his face. "Next time, ask me to hide myself." Behind him, the glow from the arrow intensified, the light seeping out onto the carpet and through the folds in the jacket.

"Why is it glowing like that," Clifton said. "Is it because you're here?"

Dane shook his head. "No. It's the princes. They have been taken again and locked up, this time in a place called Droffilc Tower." The worry lines around his eyes gave his skin a look of wet clay. "I fear King Richard will not be thwarted from his plan to execute them."

"So take the arrow back," Clifton said. "Here, I'll get it for you."

Dane grabbed Clifton by the wrist. "I can't. It's not the arrow I seek."

Clifton's pulse quickened. Fearing the inevitable, he asked, "Then why are you here, Dane?"

The little man looked up with pleading blue eyes. "I've come to bring ya back, lad. The princes need yer help."

Chapter Fifteen
Fated

"**W**hat do you mean; the princes need my help?" Clifton asked.

"Can't be much clearer, boy. They're locked up, and that thing's a-glowing." He pointed toward the arrow. "Seems yer connected to all this. Why in the blazes it chose you, I'll never know."

"Thanks a lot."

"No offense, lad. But yer not the sharpest nail in the shed, the brightest coal in the fire, the--"

"Okay, I get it. You sure do know how to give a good pep talk."

Dane stared at him. "Charm ain't one of me defining features."

"You can say that again."

Stepping inside his closet, Clifton lifted the heavy winter coat that now concealed the arrow. He covered his eyes from the white light burning brightly in the darkness and set the arrow on his bed. Feathers rippled. The shaft glowed. Its diamond tip shook. Loitering near his bookshelf, his fingertips tracing the spines, Clifton took down a file wedged deep between his books for safekeeping. He opened it, spreading the printed documents across his bed. "I studied what happened in 1485." He dragged his words. "It seems to me that the princes disappeared after they were left in the Tower of London."

"Aye. Not many souls know of their escape."

"There's more, though. In history, they were left for dead." Clifton shook his head. "I don't know, Dane. I mean, what if that's their fate? Chosen or not, it's not my place to interfere."

Stepping over to the bed, Dane glanced at the documents, pausing to read segments from Clifton's research. He stopped at a copy of the oil painting. Carefully, he lifted it, staring at the face of the boy among the horses and men on the battlefield. He held it up to Clifton. "This is yer fate."

Clifton took a step back and shook his head. "No. It's not possible. You don't know me, Dane."

"Yer right, lad. I don't know, but the arrow does." He shoved the picture into Clifton's hands.

Clifton stared at the painting, knowing the dwarf was right. Fear gripped him. He didn't want to die. He didn't want to lose his family. He didn't want to lose his future. But thinking of all the reasons why he didn't want to help wasn't enough. The faces of those two princes, forgotten by history, haunted him.

They deserved a chance to be remembered.

Clifton's shoulders slouched; acceptance stamped across his face like footprints in the sand. "I knew I'd be going back one day. Right here." Clifton pointed to his gut.

Dane smiled. "Good. Yer learning." He strode to the window and opened the shade. "Grab the arrow and hurry." Dragging the desk chair over, Dane climbed onto it and opened the window.

"What are you doing?" Clifton asked.

"Leaving. Have ya not been listening?"

"What? We're going to sneak out my window?" Clifton asked, sliding the arrow onto his back.

"Would ya prefer we use the front door?"

"No, way," Clifton said. "The window's fine."

"All right then. Follow me."

The dwarf lifted his stout body over the ledge, leg over leg, landing in the bushes below the window. He crept around the perimeter of the house, the top of his head disappearing beneath the shrubs.

"Here we go again," Clifton said, stepping out, closing the window quietly behind him.

Chapter Sixteen

Back

C lifton followed Dane through his yard, hiding in the shadows of trees. Dusk disappeared, replaced by a deep purple night. He whispered, "So, what's the plan?"

"We walk."

Dane stopped near a rotating sprinkler-head, precisely timing his movement so as not to get wet. Clifton, however, fell behind and caught the tail-end of the spray. He puffed his cheeks and caught up to Dane. "I hate to point out the obvious," Clifton said, "but we can't exactly walk to England from here. And I don't know how to work the time-travel part of the arrow."

Dane kept pressing through neighboring yards, the crunch of crabgrass beneath his boots his only response.

"You know, my parents will start looking for me if I'm gone for longer than an hour."

Dane stopped short. "Blasted, boy. Dontcha ever shut up? I got myself here, dontcha think I can get us back without yer knowing all the details?" He turned and kept marching, leaving a slightly wet, slightly embarrassed Clifton to follow him.

The streetlights lit their way across Elm, then Maple, and the houses in between the blocks, until they exited Clifton's neighborhood. Hugging the bushes off the main intersection, they ran in spurts between the empty spaces where no shadows could cover them.

"There," Dane said. "To the field up ahead."

Fern Park marked the edge of Clifton's neighborhood. It included a covered playground, shuffleboard court, and large soccer field surrounded by industrial lights for night games. They crossed the lit parking lot and headed to the dark field. Clifton thought the city kept the lights on for a few hours after dark but couldn't remember. Looking over his shoulder, he noticed darkness canopied the parking lot.

Hadn't the lights been on a second ago?

A yellow moon rose, and twinkling stars stretched across the sky. The night air cooled the blacktop. Cicadas shrieked shrill songs in the tall grasses growing against the wooden fence that ran the perimeter of the field. The dwarf slipped in between two boards while Clifton climbed over them. When he reached midfield, Dane stopped short.

Clifton looked around. "Why are we stopping?"

Silently, Dane stared up into the night sky without answering.

Clifton laid down on the soft turf, gazing at the stars in search of constellations to pass the time. He could only make out the Big Dipper. Frustrated, he pushed up onto his elbows. "What are we doing here, Dane? I'm gonna be in so much trouble for sneaking out. Especially since the last thing I did was fight with my dad."

Dane continued his unbreakable trance with the sky.

Clifton stood. "I'm heading home. Thanks for nothing."

As Clifton treaded back to the fence, Dane said, "Wait. She'll be here any second."

Clifton turned. "Who?"

"The one to take us back."

A loud flapping of what had to be enormous wings rustled the still sky. Clifton rushed back to Dane's side. "What is that?" he asked.

"You mean who is that," Dane said with his crooked, little smile.

A great bird, the size of a hundred birds, circled to land, with large fans of air sweeping off her wings as huge gusts of wind. Fiery red plumes dragged behind her on the current, copper-colored feathers that shimmered with veins of golden highlights.

Clifton gasped. "Is that Simurgh?"

"Aye, lad. She is here to take us back."

Simurgh landed, her talons digging into the soccer turf while soft pads, like a lion's, pushed her along. Feathers, similar to the tail of a peacock, swept off her dog-head. Her massive body expanded and contracted with each deep breath she took.

"Hello, Clifton Chase," Simurgh sang.

Clifton stared at the face of a beautiful woman whose features embedded in a dog-head. High cheekbones, pale lips, crystal eyes shining in an unknown shade similar to violet. She was like an old friend he'd known his whole life while also the most awe-inspiring creature he'd ever laid eyes upon.

"It is my honor to meet you." She bowed her head low.

Clifton nodded, his mouth suddenly sandpaper, and he croaked, "Nice to meet you, ma'am."

Gracefully, she stretched her wing like an angled ladder against the ground. Dane pushed Clifton toward it.

"Well, whatcha waiting for? Climb aboard."

Clifton turned. "Seriously?"

"No, lad. She's here to make company. Of course, I'm serious."

Clifton hesitated, reaching out to touch Simurgh's wing. Her feathers pressed between his fingers like the fletching on the Arrow of Light.

How could this be real?

"Go ahead, Clifton," Simurgh said. "Take hold."

He clutched a handful of feathers, and Simurgh lifted him gently onto her back. He rubbed her down, like the softest pillow he'd ever touched. Dane climbed up and settled in front of Clifton, taking hold of both sides of Simurgh's broad back. His face grimaced. Clifton gripped Simurgh with soon-to-be white-knuckled fists as Simurgh sprung off the ground. His eyes clenched as cool air rushed over his face as she flew higher.

"Open your eyes," he told himself. He opened them and found he was several hundred feet up, the city flickering like strung Christmas lights beneath him. He smiled, then laughed, and couldn't stop even if he wanted to. "This is amazing!" he shouted to Dane, whose head was still buried in Simurgh's feathers.

Clifton loosened his grip as they flew higher. Below him, the ground looked like a grid with varying shades of squares and rectangles hopping across lakes and rivers. The higher they flew, the more the shapes and shades merged into a splotchy paint pallet of earth and water. As they passed through misty clouds, Clifton shivered, unable to see through the fog. Simurgh charged higher, unswayed. Eventually, they cleared the clouds and were basking in space, surrounded by more stars than Clifton knew existed, twinkling through the atmosphere like millions of bright eyes winking at him.

Suddenly, lights streamed all around him rapidly growing in speed and intensity, the air both impeding and intrusive at the same time. Sound mirrored the air by growing thunderous then silent while colors whirled, many of which Clifton had never seen before; shades mixed unexplainably, like Simurgh's violet-hued crystal eyes.

Pressure swirled, pinning him to Simurgh's back. He screamed noiselessly, wincing, his blood trying to push out of his veins like the last bit of toothpaste squeezed against a capped-off tube. And when he thought he couldn't take another second of it, everything stopped, and they were floating again above the misty clouds, beneath the full moon and twinkling stars.

Chapter Seventeen
Simurgh

"That was awesome!" Clifton yelled. "What a rush."

Dane lifted his head, his face pale, his fists still grasping Simurgh's back. "If ya like that sort of a thing."

"Where are we?" Clifton asked.

"The question you should be asking is *when* are we," Simurgh replied. "Where one is can be useless information if one does not know when one is."

"I've never needed to think about that before." Clifton shook his head. "Do you always speak in riddles?"

"It is only a riddle to you because you do not know the answer to either question, neither where nor when." Simurgh began her descent through the clouds.

"Okay," Clifton said. "Then, when are we?"

"You have returned to the year 1485, though it is now late summer. I believe it was spring when you last visited."

Clifton's forehead scrunched. "How is that possible? I only left a few days ago."

"Many things are possible when they are not questioned," Simurgh responded.

They emerged through the clouds. The rising sun lit the green fields and treetops. A mountain range spanned for miles in the distance. Blue-gray waterways wound like the fingers of a giant.

"Are we back in York?" Clifton asked, not recognizing the geography.

"Not quite," Dane said. "We are over the Elan Valley in Wales. Down below, ya can see the Elan River leading to Birmingham."

Clifton spied the churning river and streams, the bogs and oak woodlands punctuating the hillside. Small bushes reminded him of green cotton balls on construction paper like Pierce made in kindergarten.

"How did we get here?" Clifton asked Simurgh. "I mean, how can you break laws of physics and time?"

"I am without time and space constraints," Simurgh said, flying lower and lower to the ground. "I was created before Time herself and thus can enter and leave her boundaries at my leisure, a courtesy I have extended to you both."

The land sharpened into view as Simurgh flew closer. Clifton noticed a lake, a forest of fir trees, and a village with small thatched roof houses angling up the stony ledge of the mountain.

Simurgh approached the lake, its banks and water plants growing more defined. Simurgh landed softly, considering her enormous size. "We will rest here," she said, lowering her left wing to the ground. "I must drink."

Clifton and Dane climbed off the great bird's back. Simurgh approached the lake's edge and lowered her face, lapping the water in hungry gulps with her canine tongue. Using his cupped hands, Clifton sipped cold water until quenching his thirst. He stood and stretched. His stomach growled. "I sure am hungry. Wish I had grabbed my dinner before we left."

Dane closed his eyes and sat in the shade of a large tree. Clifton stood over the little man for a few seconds before clearing his throat. "Yup. Sure am hungry."

The dwarf didn't stir.

Clifton sighed heavily. "If only I'd had a chance to eat before I was rushed out. Maybe I wouldn't feel so completely famished and weak." He smiled, waiting for Dane to give into his dramatics.

The dwarf still didn't stir.

"I think my stomach is eating itself. It's barking; I'm so hungry."

Shaking his head, Dane said, "Why don't ya look above us and shut up already."

Clifton tilted back his head, noticing green apples hanging from the boughs. "Oh, thanks. Didn't see those."

"Obviously," Dane mumbled.

Clifton picked off two apples then shook Dane by the shoulder. "Dane, you hungry?"

The dwarf opened one eye. "I'm fine," he said through gritted teeth.

"Suit yourself." Clifton ate the fruit in large bites, reached the core, and bit into the second piece. "So, what's next?"

The dwarf grunted. "Well, I was hopin' to rest me eyes, but it seems you intend to yap me to death." He opened his sack and handed Clifton a wadded up pile of clothes. "Here. Put these on."

"What are these?"

"Clothes, lad. Can't very well be seen wearing the garments ya be wearing. And these, too." He tossed Clifton the pair of hide boots he had worn the last time.

Clifton stepped behind a large mulberry bush, popping tart berries in his mouth while he changed. "What's up with all these clasps?" he asked, attaching the pants to the shirt like before. "Zippers are a whole lot easier. Especially when you have to…you know."

"Know what?" Dane called.

"Take a leak."

Clifton heard Dane shift, then holler, "How do you take a leak, lad? What are ya yakking about?"

"Forget it," Clifton said, finishing up. He wondered if he should bother packing his own clothes considering they had found their way onto him after his last visit, when he had exited the lake at Wickham Park. He decided to pack them, just in case.

"How do I look?" Clifton asked, walking as if he were modeling for Tommy Hilfiger's medieval campaign.

"Terrible," Dane said with a crooked smile. "By the looks of your face, ya must'ave cleaned that whole bush of berries."

Clifton looked at his hands and wiped his mouth, the purple stain too deep to make a difference.

"Now stop parading yerself and come sit down for lunch."

Dane handed him crusty bread with cheese that smelled like dirty feet but tasted like a slice of heaven. "Man, the food here is good."

Dane smiled, handing him a leather bottle. "Take this. It's from Liv."

Clifton opened the top and took a large gulp. "Dropwater? No way. Tell Liv thank you." He drank more. "I can't believe it's still warm."

"Don't drink it all, boy," Dane commanded, while Clifton drank from the tilted bottle.

Clifton lowered the Dropwater and wiped his wet mouth on his sleeve. He loaded the bottle in his pack finally ready to rest. Simurgh lay curled up, snoring gently on the bank. While she slept, her face softened like a child's.

"So, what's the plan?" Clifton asked Dane.

"The plan for what?"

"To rescue Edward and Richard."

"Yer the plan," Dane said.

"Me? I don't have the faintest idea what to do."

"Then, this could be a very long rest."

The dwarf closed his eyes, quickly falling into a deep sleep where his snores were louder than sawing wood. Clifton lay beneath the tree, watching the clouds roll past, wondering how in the world he was supposed to save the princes.

He dreamed of success, dreamed of Ava, simply dreamed…

Chapter Eighteen

Planned

Clifton stood on a ledge overlooking a vast chasm. Across from him, Dane clutched a fatal wound in his stomach. From behind, the enemy closed in. The Arrow of Light glowed vibrantly, and Clifton leapt, desperate to cross the expanse and reach Dane in time. But he wouldn't make it, couldn't make it, no matter how hard he begged the arrow to help. The open mouth of the chasm delighted in swallowing him up, and before he hit bottom…

His eyes popped open.

"You all right?" Dane asked.

Clifton sat near the lake in Wales, covered in sweat. "Yeah. Had a bad dream." He crossed downhill to the lake and splashed cool water against his face.

Simurgh stirred from her slumber appearing refreshed. She stood and shook from head to tail, ruffling her feathers where they had flattened against her body. "Much better."

Clifton sat on the bank, pushing his nightmare out of his mind. "Did you sleep well?"

"Indeed. And you?"

Clifton yawned. "I don't even remember falling asleep."

Dane joined them, clearing his throat. "Did ya come up with a plan yet?" he asked Clifton, taking a sip from his bottle.

"Me? No. I thought you were joking."

"Go on then," Dane said. "We haven't got all day."

Clifton paced, which always seemed to help him think. "Well, let's start with what we know. How did you and Jasper get them out the last time?"

"Different tower, boy," Dane said. "That was the Tower of London. This is Droffilc Tower. We need a different tactic."

"What's the place like? Have you been there before?" Clifton asked.

"I have," Dane said. "It's on a large mound, which gives the advantage to the guards. The hardest part will not be getting inside. It will be getting close enough, without being spotted so that we can get inside."

"That's a start," Clifton said. "Do you know where they're at in the tower?"

"Not precisely," Dane said.

"How about the guards? Do we know anything about them? How many, if they have shift changes, stuff like that?"

"Not particularly, no," Dane said.

Clifton stared at him with his head cocked. "Seriously?"

"Aye, lad. Seriously."

"So, basically, we have to figure out how to charge up a hill, completely exposed, and hope that we reach the top alive."

"Yes," Dane said.

"And if we do find our way inside, which probably won't happen, we'll be completely blind, guessing where the princes are and where the guards are, with no idea how many guards we could even be dealing with?"

"Yes, lad," Dane said in excitement. "It's like you've seen it already happen."

Clifton squinted his eyes, throwing his hands up. "This isn't a good thing, Dane."

"It is actually. It seems like you've come up with a plan of sorts."

Clifton turned to face Simurgh. She nodded. "It does seem that a plan is within, if you can only decipher the code you have created."

Clifton rested his hands on his hips and looked up into the sky.

How am I supposed to do that?

"Do not think too hard. Let the simplest answer present itself and take hold," Simurgh continued.

Clifton bobbed his head and resumed pacing. "Okay. So the princes are in a tower again. Why does King Richard keep choosing towers?" He turned to Dane. "They must be at the top. Why else would they be in another tower? If we knew where the princes were exactly, that would make this so much easier."

"I have been inside once before."

"You have? Why didn't you say so?"

"Was just sleeping, boy. Takes some time for me mind to wake up. Now, if memory serves, there's a winding stairwell that curves up to the top floor. If I had to guess, I would bet they're up there, somewhere."

Clifton paced again, random questions rolling around in his head. "Can we enter the tower from any other way besides the front?"

"We could scale the walls," Dane said. "But that is a timely process requiring equipment and the precision of a skilled climber, which I can assume yer not."

"No. Definitely not."

"We do have one thing on our side that Jasper and I lacked."

"What's that?" Clifton asked, desperate for any advantage in this disaster of a rescue plan.

"The element of surprise."

Clifton shook his head. "How's that? You said yourself that King Richard knows about the arrow, so he probably knows I'm here again."

"No lad, I don't believe he does this time. None of our spies have heard mention of yer whereabouts since ya left in the spring."

"That's a relief. So, what's our advantage?"

Dane leaned in, his elbow resting on his knee. "The tower should be lightly guarded."

Clifton's nose crinkled. "Why's that? Richard's nephews have already escaped once. I'd think the place would be swarming with guards."

"No, lad, that's where yer wrong. The king doesn't expect the need for many guards because everyone thinks the princes are already dead."

Clifton's face lit up. "Oh. Now I get it." He nodded, the information seeping in and setting a plan into motion. "Yes, this could actually work." He smiled at the good news.

"Are you willing then, Clifton Chase, to risk your own life to rescue the princes from the tower?" Simurgh asked, her lips taut, eyes wide.

Clifton thought about that question for a very long time. Was he ready to sacrifice his life? He had his own to live, his own family and home to return to. Maybe even Ava. He thought of his younger brother, and what lengths he would go to, without question, if Pierce was in danger. But how could he give all of that up for two boys he didn't even know? But, how couldn't he? He would want someone to do the same for him if he were trapped somewhere, especially if they had the power to do so.

"Yes, I guess I am," Clifton replied. He laughed nervously. "What other explanation is there for my being here? I must be here to save the princes."

"Your bravery is admirable," Simurgh said. She stood. "I will assist you on your quest, flying you to the woods near the grassy hill of Droffilc Tower. You will have my broad back to carry you. It will be your task to locate the princes and rescue them. Afterwards, I will find you at the highest window." She spread her wing across his back. "I will wait for you to show yourself victorious."

"I sure hope so."

"It's settled then," Dane said. "We leave at nightfall. I will help where I can, but this quest is yours to carry."

Clifton swallowed hard. Although it felt like the right thing to do, he still didn't understand why it'd been fated to him.

Was there no one in this time to complete it?

"Who is Lady Elizabeth?" Clifton asked.

Dane stared at him, his face blanching under his leathery skin. "How do ya know that name?"

Clifton shrugged. "The internet."

"The what?" Dane asked.

"It doesn't matter," Clifton said. "She's their sister, right?" Dane paused. "Dane, you forget I have access to written history. What I showed you back in my room was nothing compared to what's out there. I know all about this time and place, who's here, and even the fate of Richard III."

Dane and Simurgh exchanged glances.

"What?" Clifton asked.

"You may have read accounts of our time in your books of history and your internet," Simurgh said. "But your presence here has altered events already."

"What do you mean?"

"Those accounts may be rewritten the next time you read them, although you will be the only one to notice the change," Simurgh continued. "You cannot use your knowledge as a timeline, as if written in stone. Use that knowledge only as an outline to guide you to the answers you seek."

Clifton nodded. "Wow, this is confusing."

"It is only confusing if you allow it to be."

"Okay," Clifton said. "I'll do my best. But I still wanna know about Elizabeth. How could she let her brothers get locked up? Doesn't she care about them? I mean, I have a little brother. He's two, and he is the coolest little bro in the whole world. There's no way I would ever let anything happen to him."

Dane placed his hand on Clifton's shoulder. "She doesn't know they are alive, lad. Like the rest, she mourned their deaths when King

Richard imprisoned them. It is common knowledge that a sentence in the Tower of London is a death sentence."

"Why haven't you told her?"

"The princes wanted ta keep her safe. If she knew the truth, then she could be prey to her uncles' wrath. They didn't want anything happening to her."

Clifton's face drained of color. He had misjudged the princes completely. "I have to talk to her."

"We will go to her village on the hillside, in Hafleur, France, under your command. We will depart at once," Simurgh said, and Clifton and Dane climbed onto her back.

Chapter Nineteen
Elizabeth

S imurgh flew in a swift pattern across mountains capped with the whitest snow. Rivers and channels flowed down the sides like troughs in mud after a hard rain. They landed at the base of a mountain situated in southern France. The Village of Èze angled up the ledge, climbing over the rocky terrain. A defensive wall of rough gray stones protected the city from intruders. As the three pressed closer to the gate, the gatekeeper stiffened, eyeing what must have appeared to be quite a strange trio.

"Who goes there?" he asked, his voice cracking, as Simurgh led closer.

"We seek audience with Lady Elizabeth of York," Dane said.

"For what purpose?" he asked. He wore a brown tunic embossed with a Phoenix perched on a bone. His face seemed baby-soft and smooth. His bald head reflected the sun. Two men appeared from behind the gatehouse joining the gatekeeper; both dressed in similar tunics and hemp pants.

"What's the problem?" the burlier of the two asked. His eyes widened, and he leaned back to take in all of Simurgh.

"Something we can help with?" the light-skinned man with freckles added, stepping behind the other as he caught sight of the great bird.

Several young women, gathering water from the well, stopped pulling on the rope to watch the activity at the gate. The older women, seated in the courtyard turning clay pots, began to murmur. Clifton assumed Simurgh was known only in name, like Godzilla. He tried to imagine what it would be like to have a mutant lizard show up at his doorstep.

The great bird inched closer to the gatekeeper. "I am Simurgh, crafted by the Creator before Time, and given a home in the Tree of the Knowledge of Good and Evil. I have received audience in the courts of King Solomon, where we exchanged the wisdom of the ages. I have seen the creation of the Earth and far ahead to its destruction. There is not much of the world and the hearts of men that I do not already know." She had passed through the gate and turned to face her comrades. "Alas, it is not I who seek audience, rather I am a servant of the one here for that purpose."

The gatekeeper drew in a breath to speak, when the burlier man shouted out, "Who then?"

The gatekeeper glared at him, apparently annoyed by his insubordination.

"Me," Clifton said, stepping forward. "I need to speak with her."

"About what?" Freckles asked, followed by another glare from the gatekeeper.

Clifton felt his throat constrict. He looked to Simurgh, who nodded with a smile. "About her brothers," he said.

A gasp rippled through the crowd. Many whispers followed. Younger women led their small children by the hand to safe places. Older woman shook their heads, clacking their tongues.

"Have you no respect?" Freckles asked.

The gatekeeper snapped. "Lady Elizabeth's brothers are dead.

She would not want to be subjected to those painful memories again."

Simurgh back peddled to the gatekeeper, her breath on his face. "It would not be prudent, my fine man, to speak on the Lady's behalf when she is not here to confirm nor deny your words."

Her eyes glowed hot, and her feathers ruffled out all around her causing her to appear very, very large. She raised her lovely lips in a snarl, exposing sharp canine teeth. A growl permeated from deep in her throat.

The gatekeeper took a step back, his eyes panicked like a wounded deer, his head nodding. He no longer appeared capable of defending the gate. He looked around him, but Freckles and Burly hid behind the women at the well. "You may enter," he said, ushering Dane and Clifton in. "I will announce you at once."

"Thank you," Clifton said, and although Dane only huffed, they passed through the gate and entered Èze.

With her feathers relaxing against her back, Simurgh bowed to the man. "You are wise," she said. "And the Lady is fortunate to have you in her service."

The man nodded, keeping his gaze on Simurgh.

Word spread quickly up the mountainside, a wave of chatter preceding the three visitors. It seemed the whole village had turned out to see the Great Simurgh for themselves, stately following the stout, redheaded dwarf guarding the boy.

A boy who remained unnamed.

A boy whom nobody knew.

Clifton looked ahead, hoping no one could hear his pounding heart. Could they tell how inadequate he was for this task? He could. He had never felt like such a child. His forehead dripped sweat. His face felt hot. He forged up the mountain, his thoughts fighting for attention at the forefront of his mind.

The narrow cobblestone streets clacked beneath Simurgh's claws, with the sound echoing hollowly off the tall buildings. They rose higher and higher on the slope, and Clifton looked out over the city wall. The view stole his breath, the greens and golds of the Mediterranean Sea glittering in the sun.

"It is beautiful," Simurgh said.

"Yeah, it really is."

"As we journey, we will pass the oldest building in Èze, called the Chapelle de la Sainte Croix," Simurgh said. "I witnessed its construction in 1306, a magnificent site with its bell-turret. I remember the bell pealing out for the first time across the countryside." She smiled, and Clifton imagined she had much to reminisce over in her long life.

They passed the chapel. Clifton noticed a sign posted over the door, stamped in what looked to be French text. Pointing, he asked, "What does that say?"

"It says, *Isis Moriendo Renascor*," Simurgh replied.

Clifton squinted. "Translation, please?"

"*In death, I am reborn*," Dane said. "It's the creed of the Phoenix."

"Why is it on a church?"

"It is the motto of the village," Simurgh said. "Its people have experienced many trials and tribulations, yet they still manage to rebuild. This is a place of great resilience."

They finally reached the top, where villagers crowded to greet them in front of the building.

"The Great Hall," Dane whispered as if reading Clifton's mind.

The doors of the Great Hall opened, and a young girl exited. Clifton recognized her at once. Her long, blonde hair fell in waves across her shoulders, just like Ava's. She smiled, and Clifton couldn't keep his eyes off her.

Clifton stopped, with Dane and Simurgh behind him, and the girl remained at the top of the stairs surrounded by armed soldiers wearing the same tunic as the gatekeeper. Their faces shared fearful expressions as they ogled Simurgh. Boy, was Clifton glad she was on his side. He took a tentative step forward. "Are you Lady Elizabeth?"

"I am she whom you seek."

Clifton nodded, trying to remember the proper way to make an introduction. They never taught that sort of stuff at school. There was no class called: How to make Introduction to Royalty-101. Or maybe he missed the semester when it was offered. He plowed right in. "My name is Clifton Chase, and these are my friends." He motioned behind him. "The dwarf is Dane Englewood of Griffon Forest."

Dane bowed. "Your Majesty."

"And she is Simurgh, but I'm guessing she doesn't need any introduction," Clifton said.

"A pleasure as always, My Lady," Simurgh said with a low bow.

"And from what land do you hail, Clifton Chase?"

Clifton rubbed the back of his neck. "I'm from Florida, a place called Melbourne."

Lady Elizabeth floated down the short flight of steps while the ladies in her attendance straightened the train of her yellow dress. "You seek audience with me, and it shall be granted."

"Thank you, My Lady," Clifton said with a smile.

Elizabeth took Clifton's hand in her own. She moved in closely; her green irises edged in gold. Her skin smelled like honeysuckles. "They say you bring word of my brothers."

"Yes, I do—," Clifton said.

She placed her rose-tinted cheek against his. Her warm breath tickled his ear. "I pray they are still alive."

Clifton squeezed her hand. She pulled back, and he nodded. Elizabeth beamed. "Then let us enter the Great Hall at once." She turned, climbing the steps, followed by her attendants and guards.

Clifton faced his friends.

"Your quest has begun," Simurgh said. "I shall return at nightfall." And she leapt into the air, flapping huge wings that carried her through the sky.

The crowd gasped, then resumed their chattering. Probably the kind of thing that would get passed down from generation to generation, the way Clifton's grandma liked to retell where she was the day JFK died.

Dane looked to Clifton. "Hurry up, lad, and get inside. I'm famished."

Clifton followed the guards into the Great Hall, overwhelmed and excited at the same time, passing the crowd staring at him.

Chapter Twenty

The Great Hall

C lifton drew in a sharp breath. He had never been inside a
building as beautiful as the Great Hall. Rectangles of white
light shone through the windows, catching the copper and
silver veins in the marble floor. Large murals spanned the ceiling
portraying men and women in stiff poses, wearing starched
powdered wigs and formal clothing. He passed towering
pillars, an expressionless guard stationed at each one. The
arched wooden doors closed with a heavy pull behind him, and two
guards manned their posts.

Lady Elizabeth glided barefoot across the cold marble, her pale
gown gently brushing her legs. She reached the raised platform at
the end of the long hall, where two thrones, inlaid with gold and
heavy metal studs, sat empty. A man with thin lips stood beside
her. Blond hair fell out of his pointy hat in course waves above the
drawn curves over his rich brown eyes. He looked at least ten years

older.

"My Lord," Elizabeth said with a curtsey. She rose on tiptoes to whisper in his ear, and he nodded with a smile. She gestured toward her guests. "May I present Clifton Chase of Florida from the place called Melbourne, and his companion, Dane the Dwarf of Griffon Forest."

Dane and Clifton bowed at their introduction. Clifton started to straighten, but Dane cleared his throat. Clifton peeked over. Dane held his bow, his bulbous nose inches from the floor. Clifton bowed farther, waiting for his next instruction.

Lady Elizabeth addressed her guests. "May I present Henry VII of Tudor, son of Edmund Tudor and Margaret Beaufort, servant to the true king of England, Edward IV and his descendants."

Henry nodded purposefully from Dane to Clifton, then to Elizabeth. Clifton's arms shook from being held out so long, his neck craning to keep his eyes focused on Henry and Elizabeth. He started to stand and again the dwarf's exaggerated throat clearing alerted him that he'd better not. Clifton lowered even farther, his back aching from the tension.

Then, Henry finally said, "You may rise."

Clifton straightened quickly, stretching his back and neck, anxious for the formal introductions to be over so he could finally act normal again.

Henry rested, which by his pose must have been in an awfully uncomfortable throne. Elizabeth waited for him to settle before sitting beside him.

"You may speak," Henry Tudor said, his face rigid.

"Thank you, Sir, uh, Sire…," Clifton said. "We are in your presence…to request permission, that is, to ask for help, from Elizabeth…and yourself for…."

Elizabeth giggled. "Relax, Clifton Chase. Just speak of the tidings you bring. Tell more about my brothers."

"It's not what you're thinking," Clifton said.

Elizabeth's mouth dropped. "But you said they were alive. Are they not well?

"I don't know. They're in trouble."

Elizabeth's eyes widened and she squeezed Henry's hand.

"What sort of trouble?" Henry asked.

"They've been captured by King Richard."

Elizabeth's hands covered her mouth. Tears welled in her eyes. Shaking her head, she said, "No. Not again. Please, what assistance do you need? Anything, and it shall be granted."

Clifton shrugged. "That's the problem. I don't know what we need."

"Your uncle has locked them in Droffilc Tower," Dane said. "And we have word that he plans to execute them on the morrow."

Clifton eyed Dane. "What?"

"No, this can't be the news you have brought me? That my brothers are alive, but soon will be dead. Why have you come?" She was breathing heavily, her face splotched red.

Clifton looked away. He had nothing left to tell her.

"Milady," Dane said. "There is hope."

She looked to Dane. "What hope can there be in the news you bring?"

Dane raised his eyebrows. "The whole countryside thinks they are already dead, including yourself, until a few moments ago."

Elizabeth's skin returned to its milky-white color. "Go on."

"I believe King Richard's own arrogance can be used against him."

"How is that?" Henry asked.

"If no one knows of the princes' whereabouts, then the tower might not be heavily guarded. Of course, Jasper and I know they are alive, but we wouldn't be dim-witted enough to rescue them twice, now would we?" He grinned.

"I see," Elizabeth said.

Clifton felt Henry eyeing him and shot him a sideways glance.

"Where do you hail from again, sir?" Henry asked.

"Uh…it's a little town called Melbourne in a state called Florida." Clifton scrunched his face imagining what it would be like to listen to a space alien explaining where he came from. "It's in a country…called America." His voice cracked.

"America?" Henry Tudor asked. "I have never heard of such a place." He shifted his weight in his seat, flinging strands of a wavy waterfall off his shoulders.

Clifton changed his footing, knowing whatever he said would sound ridiculous. "That's because it hasn't exactly been discovered yet."

"What do you mean it has not been discovered yet?"

"I mean, it won't be discovered for another seven years." His voice trailed, and he wished the ground would open up and swallow him.

"Are you a gypsy then, predicting what is to come?"

"No, Sire."

Henry's eyes narrowed. "Where is this America?"

"Straight across the Atlantic Ocean," Clifton said, pointing in any general direction, "'til you hit land."

Henry Tudor exploded with laughter. His whole body shook, the pointy hat jumping up and down. "What a tale you have spun, my young friend. There is nothing out there but the edge of the earth. You would no sooner fall off, if you managed to avoid the whirlpools and sea serpents." He turned to Elizabeth. "I had no idea this child was a jester. What a pleasant surprise."

Clifton's blood stirred; his hands fisted at his sides. "Sire?"

A smiling Henry Tudor turned to him. "Yes, child."

"I mean this with the greatest respect, but there is no edge to the earth. And I'm not sure about whirlpools because I've seen some pretty crazy stuff on Discovery Channel, but the sea serpent thing is definitely not true. They'd have found some proof with sonar by now."

"Clifton, that'll be enough," Dane said.

"You see, Sire, the world is really round. A man named Christopher Columbus will prove this and discover America in the year fourteen-ninety-two."

"Columbus?" Henry said. "That buffoon! Are you honestly telling me you believe his nonsense about the world being round?"

"Yes, Sire. In fact, I know it's true. And so will you--"

"Clifton!" Dane said, through gritted teeth. "The task at hand."

Clifton stared at Dane, suddenly realizing the absurdity of his conversation. He had not been brought here to argue. "I'm sorry. This is difficult for me." Henry's hard expression softened, and Elizabeth stared at him with a sweet look in her eyes. "Really, I don't expect any of you to understand my world. I don't understand yours at all or why I'm in it. Ever since I found the Arrow of Light, it's been—"

"The arrow?" Elizabeth interrupted, leaning forward. "Do you have it with you?"

"Of course, I do. It's the reason I'm here." He removed his backpack and opened it. Guards unsheathed their weapons stepping forward reactively. Henry Tudor gestured for them to remain at their stationed positions.

Clifton lifted the Arrow of Light and stepped to the platform, holding it out to Henry and Elizabeth. The shaft glowed, its light reflecting off their faces like a diffused spotlight.

"It is the Arrow of Light," Elizabeth said, stepping off her throne and moving closer to Clifton.

"It is our honor," Henry said, standing beside Elizabeth, and they both bowed.

Clifton stared down at the two crowns bowing before him. He turned to Dane, not expecting to see the dwarf kneeling alongside them. Slowly, Clifton turned in a circle, taking in the unexpected sight of every guard in the Great Hall kneeling. "Woah." Clifton said.

The Great Hall remained quiet and still. Not one guard moved. Only the shaft's copper-colored feathers flitted in an unseen breeze.

Henry lifted his eyes, staring into Clifton's. "You shall have all you ask for."

Chapter Twenty-One
Flight

E lizabeth and Henry joined Clifton and Dane outside the Great Hall. It was late, and a cold, white moon shone in the clear sky. Simurgh soared toward the Great Hall, her dark shadow crawling down the mountains, then spreading like a blanket over the valley. She landed, resting her left wing against the ground, awaiting her riders.

Elizabeth turned to Clifton. "These are for you." She handed him a woven quiver filled with arrows and a small bow.

Clifton nodded, taking the gift, his mouth suddenly dry. "Thank you." He opened his pack, taking out the Arrow of Light and setting it in the center of the quiver before crossing the leather band around his torso.

Elizabeth took his hands. "You remind me of my brother, Edward. He too is brave and clever." She winked. "I do not doubt your ability to bring my brothers home to me."

Clifton squeezed her hands. "I'll do my best."

She wrapped her arms around his neck. "Be careful."

"Clifton," Henry said. "These are for you." He handed him a small blade with the Phoenix of Èze etched in the handle and a belt. "We are counting on you both."

With damp palms, Clifton took the gift, strapping the belt around his waist and sliding the blade in its sheath. His backpack no longer seemed necessary, carrying only his clothes and a few items from home.

Home.

The only reason to carry the pack now was its connection to home, and although it would only weigh him down, he wasn't ready to cut those ties.

"We won't letcha down," Dane responded.

Clifton climbed up Simurgh's stiff left wing and settled on her back, followed by Dane.

"You ready, lad?" Dane asked.

Clifton looked down at Elizabeth. "As ready as I'll ever be."

Gripping large handfuls of feathers, Dane said, "Best hold on tight, then."

Simurgh leapt into the air, and Clifton nearly lost his breath. Instantly, they soared up through the cool, night air close enough to the stars that Clifton felt he could reach out and touch them. Wind rushed past them; a whistle interrupted only by the intermittent flapping of Simurgh's great wings.

"How far away is Droffilc Tower?" Clifton asked.

"Talk slower!"

Clifton repeated his question, drawing out each syllable, elevating his voice to battle the wind.

"One hour!" Dane replied in the same manner.

"Really?" Clifton thought about this for a long time. Finally, he asked, drawn out and loud, "But I thought Simurgh was beyond time!"

Simurgh's clear voice came out without strain, a thought arriving in Clifton's mind. "My relationship with Time is fragile. I can enter and exit her realm whenever I please, without restriction. Unlike you who experience time in a forward trajectory on a linear path, Time bends for me, allowing exits and entrances with ease."

"So, you can't manipulate time once you're in it, only the going and the coming?" Clifton asked though it felt more like a thought.

"Precisely," he heard again in his mind. "Once in a specific time, I cannot manipulate the rules. I am at Time's mercy, as are you, making this journey one hour long."

One hour.

An entire hour to face an onslaught of questions. Flying on a mythical creature to save two princes who could be dead, in a time completely out of his sphere of knowledge or understanding. And why? Because an arrow chose his fate? But that wasn't all true. He agreed to come back. He agreed to save the princes. No one forced him to sneak out of his bedroom, though he couldn't imagine how hysterical his parents must be with him being gone for over a day now.

Unless, of course, it was happening the same as last time. What felt like days on Clifton's last trip had only been thirty minutes in his time. Is that how this worked? Weaving in and out of bent time cost only thirty minutes of linear time? If that happened, his parents would probably never notice he'd gone missing, unless his mom came back to check on him. But with thirty minutes to kill, he could come up with all sorts of things to throw her off, like saying he went to the bathroom or to the kitchen for a drink of water and they must have missed each other. He knew it was thin, and though she might question it, he figured she'd relent in the end.

It's not like he could tell them the truth. They would never believe him. He'd be better off telling them he sneaked out to toilet-paper the neighborhood or pour bleach on the plants in front of Ryan Rivales' house, although he had no idea where the kid lived. At least that way, he would feel justified when the punishment came.

But no.

This reality seemed much worse. Being grounded until thirty sounded like a vacation when compared to what Clifton was headed for. No matter how he spun it—no matter how magical the arrow supposedly was or how unbelievable his being in England—he knew he might not have to decide whether or not to lie to his parents or tell them the truth.

Because he knew he might not live through the night.

Chapter Twenty-Two
Droffilc Tower

"**W**ake up," Dane said.

Clifton opened his eyes and lifted his head as a wispy limb, near the top of a tree, smacked him in the face.

"Ouch!" He ducked, avoiding another beating as Simurgh weaved through trees to land. He pressed his face down into her feathers, seeking safety from the attacking branches.

"We're here," Dane said.

Slowly, Clifton lifted his head, relieved to be free of the battering canopy of limbs. He dismounted, hidden by the same dense tree-line planted to protect Droffilc Tower from invaders.

For her size, Simurgh moved with incredible cat-like stealth, blending into the shadows, moving on padded paws in near silence. Even her soft pants blended with the whispers of the wind and the noises of the night.

The plan couldn't be simpler. Just climb through the tower unnoticed, get the princes, and escape through an open window where Simurgh would be hovering, waiting for them. Piece of cake, assuming Dane's theory held about the number of guards.

They crept to the edge of the glade. At their angle, the door remained out of sight, so they slid through the branches to gain a better vantage point. Laughter cut through the still air. Clifton crouched behind Dane, watchful. As far as he could tell, only two men stood guard at the entrance, passing a flask between them.

Clifton slanted his head back, taking in the height of the piled gray bricks. A shiver crept up his craning neck. How scared the princes must be, awaiting their execution, hoping Jasper and Dane would be able to save them again.

"Hold back, lad," Dane whispered. He was practically leaning on the dwarf's shoulders.

The guards separated, one stumbling down the grassy knoll, the other falling into the front door of Droffilc Tower. Clifton turned to the stumbling man taking a leak several yards from his guard post, singing to the night.

"Now!" Dane said, hustling away.

Clifton pushed up, running full force across the open field and up the grassy knoll to the tower. He pressed his back against the stone wall beside Dane, breathing heavily. Looking down the knoll, he could no longer see the first guard.

"Move," Dane said.

They made a beeline around to the front. The moonlight tinted the grass and the River Foss behind the tower. Stopping, they peered around the corner. The guard leaned against the door, his body teetering, his eyelids askew as he continued to sing very badly. He took another swig from the flask; his neck stretched to catch even the last few drops.

Dane took a small reed from his pack and placed one end to his lips. With a snap, he compressed his lungs, sending a slender dart through the air, that wedged deep into the guard's neck.

The guard gasped, dropped the flask, and lifted his hand to his neck, surveying the darkness. Pulling his hand away, he stared at his bloody fingertips. "Who the—" he gasped, and then slumped to the ground.

"C'mon," Dane said, rushing forward.

Clifton shadowed him to the door. He stared at the slouched man, hoping he wasn't dead.

Dane nudged the guard with his toe. He didn't stir. "Don't worry, lad. He's not dead. Just be unable to move fer a while."

"What happened to him?" Clifton asked, now noticing his moving chest.

"Poison, lad. It's in the tip of the arrow. Something Jasper taught."

Nice. A Medieval tranquilizer gun.

Dane removed his sword, a crazed look in his eyes. "Let's go save the princes."

Forcing a gulp down his dry throat, Clifton clenched his sheathe while Dane opened the door. It groaned, warning of intruders. They entered the quiet, dark tower.

Too quiet.

Clifton tracked the dwarf, keeping an eye behind them to make sure no one had followed. Dane maneuvered through the front hallway and down the first corridor, using the light from the burning oil sconces and the moonlight drifting in through openings in the stones. The chilly night air seeped in, cooling Clifton's sweat-covered skin. Dane stopped short, one of his hands lifted in a fist. Clifton jerked to a halt.

Laughter ricocheted off the stone walls, coming from farther down the hall. Dane motioned them forward, and they pressed on, reaching the base of the winding stairwell, where the voices grew louder. Shadows of several guards spread across the wall in the large open room off to the side. Clifton held his breath, stagnant behind the covering of the stairs.

"Here we go, lad," Dane said, in a whisper. "Now, when ya climb, don't look back, no matter whatcha hear."

"Okay." Clifton removed the knife from his belt.

"Go," Dane said, sauntering toward the room.

Clifton shot up the stairs two at a time.

"Hello, gentlemen," Dane said, his voice lagging in the distance.

The commotion of men's voices and chairs scraping the stone floor drifted into the background as Clifton climbed the eternal winding staircase. Dane's threats and insults became whispers the closer Clifton came to the top floor. He prayed Dane could outwit and evade the guards. He hoped they were drunk enough to be easily overpowered.

Clifton climbed the last few steps and leaned against the wall to recover. He poked his head around the corner. The hallway spanned both directions with only three doors to choose from. The one to his right was closed. The one to his left was open. And the one nearest him had a small wooden square etched near the top.

The cell door.

Clifton eyed the corridor before leaving the sanctuary of the stairwell. The coast seemed clear. Quietly, he approached the heavy oak door and shook the handle. It was locked. He slid the wooden rectangular covering aside. It revealed several slender bars inside a crude peephole, allowing Clifton to see the princes inside the cell. They slept on stone slab benches inside a room not much bigger than Clifton's walk-in closet. Using the faint light, he focused his eyes on their chests, watching the rise and fall of each breath. One last time, he glanced down both ends of the hall and over his shoulder to the stairs. Seeing no one, he pressed against the peephole and said, "Your Majesty."

Neither boy stirred.

"Psst… Edward," Clifton said louder, turning to check the stairs and down both halls again.

Still clear.

Edward changed positions but didn't wake up.

"Edward!" Clifton nearly shouted.

Edward opened his eyes and jumped to his feet, the sudden movement stirring Richard, who sat up on the bench, unsteady but alert.

"Over here. It's me, Clifton Chase. I've come to rescue you."

Edward pressed his face to the bars. Clifton could only see his ashen eyes.

"Clifton, thank heavens," Edward said, his voice muffled through the wood. "I am more than happy to see you."

"Where's the key?"

"The corridor to your left will lead to the guard's station. The key should be there."

"What about the guards?"

"They will be in there as well, but it is late in the night, and they drink quite a large quantity of mead here. There is not much else for them to do."

Clifton nodded, his eyes trailing down the hall, wondering what lay in wait for him.

He turned back to Edward. "Any idea where they keep the key?"

"I am sorry, no."

"I know where," Richard said.

Edward looked back at his little brother.

"Upon entering the cell, I glanced down the corridor. The guard's door stood opened, and I watched one of the guards remove the key from under a desk before catching my stare and closing the door."

Edward ruffled his little brother's hair. "Always the nosey one, aren't you?"

"But brother, that is where the guard is. It will be impossible to enter that room without notice."

Clifton looked over his shoulder again. Still no guards coming up the stairs. He hoped Dane was all right, but now wasn't the time to think about that. If he didn't find a way to get the princes out, whatever happened to Dane wouldn't matter anyway. He faced Edward. "Then let's make him notice. On our terms."

Edward pressed up to the opening again. "In what fashion?"

"I'll need you to distract the guard."

Chapter Twenty-Three
Distraction

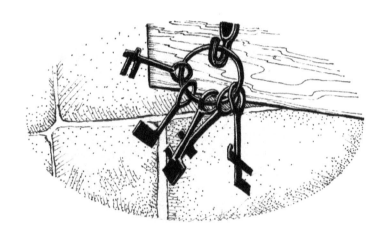

"A distraction. What a brilliant idea," Richard said.

"Exactly how can we do that from in here?" Edward asked.

"Count to five slowly. Then, call the guard over. That should give me enough time to hide. Make up something, and it better be good, to keep him busy while I grab the key."

"Great plan," Richard said. "This is exciting!"

"I don't know if I'd go that far, Richard," Clifton said. "If it doesn't work, I'll be your new cellmate."

"It will work," Edward said. "I trust you, Clifton."

"On my lead," Clifton said. "Start counting, now..."

Clifton bounded down the short corridor to a shadowed patch beside the guard door. It seemed a tight fit, angling down and forming a triangle with the floor and the wall. Clifton crouched in the darkness, knife in hand, hoping he wouldn't have to use it.

"Guard?" Edward bellowed. "Guard!"

The guard room door swung open, and Clifton blocked his head. The hard wood banged his elbow and forearm. He dropped the knife and the metal struck the stone floor with a clank. Clifton muted it with his boot. Stopping short, the guard scanned the hallway behind him, his body rocking, his eyes glazed over.

"Guard?" Richard chimed in.

The guard continued down the corridor, swaying between the walls. "What dis it you want, you liddle bratz?" he slurred, approaching the cell door and pressing his face against the peephole's iron bars.

Clifton bounced up and into the room, pushing his knife into the sheathe. He found a wooden cup beside a half-filled barrel of mead — the desk held only a Bible. Clifton slipped his hand beneath it, feeling around for the hook. Where was it? He stole a glance over his shoulder. The guard seemed to be holding himself up by leaning against the cell door. Bending over, Clifton peeked under the desk. He found the hook, but no key. Where else could it be?

"I think I saw a rat," Clifton heard Edward say.

"A rat?" the guard said. "So, eat it. Have some meat this week." His laugh came out in a rasp, followed by a wet cough.

"Not this rat, Sir. I am afraid it did not look—well."

Clifton opened desk drawers, rummaging through while stealing glances of the guard every few seconds. Still no key.

"Bah!"

Clifton turned. The guard staggered his way, waving a condescending hand in the direction of the cell. Clifton dove under the desk, trapping himself, praying Edward sensed his danger and would continue with the charade. Clifton followed the guard's teeter-totter steps moving down the hall toward the doorway.

"Wait," Edward pleaded.

The guard stopped in his tracks.

"You do remember the plague? Do you not, Sir?" Edward asked.

The guard slowly turned, stumbling back toward the cell. "How do you mean the rodent ain't looked well?"

Clifton sighed in relief, jumping out from under the desk, snagging his hair on the key hook. He spied on them from behind the doorframe for a moment, wanting to be certain the guard wasn't coming straight back.

"Oh, not well at all," Edward said.

"It had sores all over its body," Richard added. "And I think it was missing one of its legs."

Clifton smiled and returned to his mission, searching inside the guard's shoulder bag. Empty.

"Could that happen? Could the Black Death return?" the guard asked, back against the cell door.

"One cannot be too sure," Edward said. "It has only been one hundred years since the outbreak. My mother's aunt told me stories of men walking through the streets covered in rotting flesh and burning boils. A terribly painful way to leave this world." He sent himself into a violent coughing fit. "Oh, no. I do not think I am well. How about you, Richard?"

Richard faked a horrendous sneeze. "Oh, yes. I am feeling sick all over."

"You must open the door, Sir, and catch the rat," Edward said, "before the bugger kills us all!"

"Oh, all right," the guard said.

And Clifton heard it, the faint tinkling of metal on metal. He turned, eyes gaping, mouth hanging open. The guard had the key the whole time. Fumbling with the ring, his large body swaying, the guard tried unsuccessfully to insert the key into the small keyhole.

What should he do now? Follow the guard, wait until he opened the door, then shove him in? The guard weighed a buck-seventy-five to two hundred pounds, easy. Drunk or not, that would be difficult. And although Clifton carried weapons, he wasn't sure if he could use them. Sure, he'd killed plenty of people in video games, and he'd shot tons of targets and some living animals with his bow and arrow. But a person? Could he do it?

He thought of Pierce, locked behind that door, and a surge of warmth flooded him. He had to take this guard down. Shaking, he reached into his quiver and pulled out one of the arrows from Lady Elizabeth. He trained his eyes on the guard, envisioning him as a fat deer, and fitted his bow.

He knew his arrow would launch straight.

Holding his breath, Clifton steadied his aim and pressed his fingertips to the bowstring gliding it to full draw. He squinted, then closed his eyes. "C'mon. It's now or never," he told himself, prepared to release the arrow.

When suddenly, there was a loud thump.

Chapter Twenty-Four

Great Escape

C lifton opened one eye, the arrow still notched, the bowstring against his ear.

"What happened?" Edward asked. "Did you get him?"

The guard lay face down on the ground in front of the cell door, passed out drunk. Clifton heaved a sigh, shaking from leftover adrenaline—fear and joy—at not having to kill the guard. "Of all the dumb luck," Clifton said, racing to the princes. He replaced his bow and arrow, leaned into the peephole, and said, "Piece of cake."

Edward's eyes squinted. "Now? Are you mad?"

"Never mind," Clifton replied. He lifted the guard's arm, the key in his tight grip. Carefully, Clifton loosened his fingers. The guard snorted, eyelids fluttered, and Clifton froze. The guard passed a thick, mucous-filled cough, and then continued to snore. Clifton ripped the key from his fist and unlocked the door.

The princes stepped out of the small cell and over the unconscious guard.

"What happened to him?" Richard asked.

"He passed out," Clifton said.

"That was lucky," Richard said with a smile.

"There's no such thing as luck," Edward said. "It was fated to be."

Clifton looked into Edward's grinning face. His cheeks were sunken in. Dark circles clung beneath his eyes. He looked thinner than Clifton remembered, which seemed weird because by Clifton's time it had only been a few days, but in this time, it had actually been several months. "You both okay?"

The princes nodded. "A bit hungry," Richard added.

"We'll take care of that as soon as we can," Clifton said. "Now, follow me."

Clifton led the boys down the corridor opposite the guard's room. It turned, wrapping around the stairwell, and soon opened into a terrace with three rocky windows that were big enough for each of them to fit through. Small block openings in the wall behind them showed the stairwell was still empty.

Clifton climbed the platform to the middle window and searched outside. A fog had drifted in, damp and cool, and Clifton could barely see three feet ahead. Where was Simurgh? She promised to be circling the tower, hovering outside the upper windows until Clifton and the princes appeared.

Footsteps landed hard on the stones of the winding stairwell. Clifton jumped off the platform and pressed his face to the small squares. He heard the footfalls of two guards climbing the steps. Any second now, they would find the opened cell door and the drunken guard lying lifeless on the ground.

Clifton took out his knife and handed it to Edward. "Get in the window. Hide behind the bricks for as long as you can."

"What should I do?" Richard asked.

"Get behind your brother."

Richard shifted behind Edward, who looked stiff while Clifton climbed back into the middle space and fit his bow, this time with the Arrow of Light. It glowed so brightly he worried it would attract the guards. He hoped it would attract Simurgh. Clifton glanced over his shoulder. The thick fog covered everything. He couldn't even see the moonlight. And still no Simurgh.

The guard's heavy tread turned to shuffles. They had reached the top. Clifton heard them pause, imagining them swarming into the cell and finding it empty. Then shouting and kicking, followed by slurred swearing from the guard who'd been beaten awake.

Clifton's hands grew slick with sweat, his arms quaked, and the echo of scuffing boots grew louder. The guards would round the corner soon. The shaft grew white-hot, glowing like the center of a flame, scorching the side of his face. Angry voices bounced off the stone walls. Clifton's heart pounded.

Where was Simurgh?

The infuriated guards appeared, first their shadows rounding the dark corner, then the guards themselves. This was it. Suddenly, a wind gusted through the windows, and all the sconces in the corridor blew out. The Arrow of Light extinguished. Clifton turned. The fog, so thick it could be cut, swept past him and filled the room. The guards fumbled, yelling, swearing, bumping into each other, and smacking into the stone walls.

Outside the tower, the fog had cleared, and the outline of Simurgh's large body surfaced as a hovering shadow. "At your service," she said, extending a strong wing to the window's ledge.

"It's about time," Clifton said. He placed the Arrow of Light in his quiver and hung the bow across his chest.

"I could not find you until you provided a beacon," Simurgh said.

"A beacon?"

"The arrow, it guided me through the fog to your window."

"And just in time, too," Richard said. "Let us do get out of here." He pulled himself up onto Simurgh's wing, climbing it to the top of her broad back.

"Highness," Clifton said, motioning to Edward. "Hurry up, the fog's clearing."

Edward assented, grabbing a handful of feathers, but then

stopped short. His eyes bulged and, even in the darkness, Clifton could tell the color had drained from his face.

"What's the matter?" Clifton asked.

"Brother is paralyzed by heights," Richard called down.

Edward's body turned rigid. There was no way he would be able to climb. Simurgh gently lifted Edward. He clutched her wing as if yanking out her feathers, before finally settling on Simurgh's back and letting go.

The fog screen had completely dissipated.

"There he is!" a guard yelled, nearly foaming at the mouth with rage. "Get 'em!"

Clifton turned. A large man with a scruffy beard led the pack of angry guards. "That's the one that stole the princes. King Richard will have your head."

"Simurgh!" Clifton yelled.

Simurgh's wing appeared in the window, and Clifton grabbed ahold. "Pull me up!"

She lifted her wing, dangling Clifton like a fishing lure. The guard grabbed his ankle, and Clifton stopped midair.

"Gotcha now, boy."

"Simurgh!" Clifton screamed, kicking his free foot into the side of the guard's head. The guard tightened his grip, reaching for Clifton's flailing leg. So was someone else. Clifton felt his hold on Simurgh lessening. "Simurgh, help!"

"I believe this is where you get off," Dane said, appearing at the edge of Simurgh's back.

With a quick breath, Dane pointed his reed and shot a poisoned dart into the man's arm. The guard's hold went limp and Clifton kicked free, scurrying to the safety of Simurgh's broad back. Dane reloaded and shot a dart at the second guard but missed as Simurgh flew away, high above the clouds, with the two guards shouting profane good-byes from the opening.

Clifton sprawled breathlessly across Simurgh's soft back, holding tightly with both hands. The princes sat behind him; Richard laughed; Edward panted.

Dane turned around. "Well-done, lad," he said, with a crooked smile.

"I didn't think I'd make it. When that guard had my ankle, I thought—"

"Don't matter now. You're alive and so are the princes."

"I can't believe you made it out," Clifton replied. "How did you get past the guards?"

"That be a story I'll save for another occasion," he said. "For now, catch your breath and rest. The princes are safe."

Chapter Twenty-Five

Knight

C lifton stood near a banquet table in the Great Hall. The room was lit by hundreds of candles, and large vases of fresh flowers decorated each table. He felt ridiculous, wearing a formal shirt with a ruffled collar and lacy sleeve-ends, even though every man in the room sat dressed in the same manner. Soft cotton trousers bunched beneath his knees, reminding him of pajama bottoms, though, thankfully, they didn't scratch like the hemp pants he'd been wearing since yesterday. Beneath the pants, Clifton wore maroon tights making his legs resemble beets, a detail he planned to forget if he ever told anyone about his time-travel adventure.

Lady Elizabeth, smoothing out her hair, shuffled from behind the platform toward Clifton. She reminded him of a little girl anxiously awaiting the arrival of a birthday package. Linking arms with him, she said, "I am nervous." Her eyes glittered like the greens and gold's reflecting off the Mediterranean. "And, also, very excited." She led Clifton to the head table, motioning to a seat beside Dane. A servant quickly pulled the chair out for Clifton. He sat awkwardly, trying to help by pushing himself in, but only making it more difficult for them both. Elizabeth took her place beside Henry Tudor.

Dane wore a rose-tinted shirt with lace trim and gold embroidery. He smelled like lavender from the scented bathing rag, and his slick hair was pinned in a tight ponytail. Frayed curls escaped in wispy strands.

"Don't you look pretty," Clifton said, with a smirk.

"Ya best shut up, lad," Dane replied, squirming in his seat. "Already feel like a little girl's doll. I don't need ya taunting on top of it."

Clifton laughed. "But you clean up so nice, Dane. I bet Liv would love to see you all fixed up like this."

Dane glared at Clifton. "Dontcha dare speak a word of this to Liv. If ya do, I'll… I'll…"

Clifton nodded while Dane scratched the back of his head, pulling out more strands. "I'll make ya stay here, and I'll never take ya home."

"I can find my own way home. I did last time."

Dane growled and grabbed his cup of ale, polishing it off in three large gulps.

It seemed the whole city had turned out for the prince's homecoming. Ladies in taffeta gowns, men in upturned shoes, some of which sat closest to the head table in the same itchy-looking powdered wigs as the people in the mural on the ceiling. Four trumpeters, wearing gaudy metallic tunics, marched through the hall and faced the crowd. They screeched out a sing-song melody; their cheeks puffed wide.

At the end of their piece, a pudgy squire with wiry hair entered the room. He rushed to the front and hushed the crowd. "Ladies and Gentlemen of Èze. On behalf of Henry Tudor and his betrothed, the Lady Elizabeth of York, we welcome you to the Great Hall for this special ceremony. Please rise."

Chairs pushed noiselessly across the marble floor. The guests whispered anxiously.

"Today marks a glorious occasion, one that shall find its place in the history books…"

Clifton nearly spat out his drink.

"For today, ladies and gentlemen, I present the heirs of Edward IV, Prince Richard Plantagenet of Shrewsbury and Prince Edward V of Wales." The front door opened. Light beamed in, silhouetting the two princes and their guards. "The true king of England has returned!"

The room came to life with a balcony quintet playing scales on harpsichords, bells, lyres, and tumbrels. A downpour of applause sounded, mixed with gasps, laughter, and cheers. The brothers paraded into the Great Hall, wearing silks draped with royal blue tunics and robes. Gold tassels trimmed Edward's clothing along with a raised fur collar. As the princes passed, each man bent low, and each woman curtsied, cooling their faces with elaborate fans.

Elizabeth wiped tears from her eyes, this being the first time in months she had seen her brothers, having assumed they were imprisoned in the Tower of London and left for dead. Henry clapped, but Clifton couldn't read if he were sincere, considering what it could mean for his future. The princes continued their procession to the upper platform.

"Elizabeth!" Richard said, rushing toward his sister. He fell into her arms and cried while she kissed the curls on his head. "It feels forever since I have seen you."

"My sweet, darling brother. I have been waiting for this moment for too long." They released, and Richard took his seat at the head table, wiping his eyes with his robe.

"Hello, sister," Edward said from the bottom of the platform.

She smiled. "Edward."

"It does my soul such pleasure to look upon you," he said, climbing the stairs. They held each other, and this time Elizabeth buried her face in his chest, sobbing, while Edward rocked her in his arms.

Clifton thought of Pierce and the way he would run over and jump into his arms when Clifton came home from school. He wanted more than anything right then to kiss Pierce's tiny cheeks.

The squire returned to the platform, motioning for the room to be still. "Please, please. Take your seats." Edward escorted Elizabeth to her seat. At the table, he shook hands with Henry, who pulled him into an embrace and pecked each of his cheeks, telling him something Clifton couldn't overhear.

When the music died down, and the guests were seated, Edward moved out from behind the head table on the platform. The room fell silent. After a long pause, he said, "What a wonderful day to be gathered among friends."

The crowd applauded and cheered for a brief moment. Edward motioned for them to cease. Clifton felt a sense of awe watching the people respond to Edward as their king, not as a teenaged boy.

"Many of you have mourned for my brother and I." His eyes grew weighty. "From the depths of our hearts, accept our apologies. Thank you for your loyalty to our father. We have remained in hiding for many months, hoping to keep our identities and our loved ones out of harm's way." He glimpsed at Elizabeth. "We see now that eluding King Richard is not the answer, and we pledge to stay with you from this point forward."

More applause rang through the Great Hall. Servants carried silver platters of whole pigs, garnished with dark lettuce and apples, to the banquet tables. Banquet bowls overflowed with stuffed eggplants, white fish with creamed anchovies, and chilled zucchini soup with pesto.

Edward gestured to Richard, who stood. "Before we indulge in the meal," Edward said, "my brother and I must express our thanks to one boy whose courage and wisdom are the only reasons we stand before you today."

Clifton chewed a mouthful of bread smothered in a garlicky olive oil paste, his mouth covered in a layer of grease, his breath a weapon of torture. He used his lace shirt ends for a napkin and Dane rolled his eyes. Like he wouldn't have done the same thing.

Elizabeth padded in great strides to her brother's side, followed by a long, dark-haired servant carrying a magnificent sword. The golden hilt glistened, as if breathing, the blade etched with gold and black swirls.

Edward said, "Clifton Chase of Melbourne, Florida, arise and come forth." His voice rumbled through the Great Hall.

Clifton pushed back his chair, which screeched painfully across the marble. Everyone stared. He treaded around the long head table to Edward. Clifton hoped his tights hadn't ripped. He wished he had a breath mint.

"Please kneel," Edward said.

Clifton fell to one shaky knee. Elizabeth held the great sword out to Edward, who lifted it from her outstretched palms. This close, Clifton admired the craftsmanship of the hilt, weaving gold lines evolving into a grip of twin serpents.

Holding the sword flat against his face, Edward said, "For your courage and loyalty, in the face of death, I dub thee Sir Knight."

Clifton couldn't believe it. Him? A Knight? This was awesome! And then, with a rocking that nearly knocked Clifton to the floor, Edward slapped him hard across the face. Clifton's eyes popped.

He hadn't seen that one coming.

He rubbed his cheek, wishing he had Coach Alonso's icepack, and rotated his jaw to check its alignment.

Edward's lip curled, and he reached out his hand. "You may arise, Sir Clifton."

Leery, Clifton took his hand. "I hope that's part of the ceremony and nothing personal."

Edward laughed, grabbing Clifton around his shoulder. "I will not lie and say I found no pleasure in your surprise. But honestly, Clifton, you are now my friend and as a brother."

Clifton stood taller, the pain in his cheek dismissed.

"Your sword." Edward held out the twin serpent handle. "Because of the circumstances surrounding your presence here and the unique choices you have willingly made, it is my honor to bestow upon you this sword and the legacy it upholds."

Clifton took the sword, which lay lighter in his hands than it appeared. The gold more than breathed, it seemed to reflect beyond the world around it.

"Now let us eat."

The room filled with chatter and laughter, clanking wooden cups, and clinking silverware. Edward took his seat.

Clifton stayed on the platform, reading the inscription on the blade. He swore his heart literally stopped in his chest. He read it again. Yup, it still said the same thing.

"Excuse me, Edward," Clifton said, facing the head table.

Edward looked up from his meal, a roasted duck leg in his hand.

"I'm sorry to interrupt, but..." Clifton laughed. "This sword has an inscription on it, and I swear it says—"

"Who so pulleth out this sword of this stone and anvil, is rightwise king born of England," Edward said.

Clifton stared at him, not able, or maybe not willing to believe what he had read and heard.

"It has been in our family for generations," Edward continued. "But it once belonged to a boy who was thrust into greatness as yourself."

The music played. The sword grew heavy, and Clifton's knees buckled from the pressure. The room swirled, colors and sounds, and he wondered if a time-travel portal had opened. But before everything went black, Clifton understood the magnitude of the inscription.

He was holding Excalibur.

Chapter Twenty-Six

Awakened

C lifton opened his eyes. His neck ached from sitting slouched at the head table. How long had he been out? Across the room, the attendees for the princes' homecoming celebration danced to the upbeat music of the quintet. Clifton lifted his head and winced.

"Welcome back, lad," Dane said, slurping fish soup.

"What happened?" Clifton asked, rubbing the back of his head.

"Ya went down like a sack of potatoes." Dane laughed. "Knocked yer head on the platform's steps and dropped the sword on Prince Edward's toe."

"That explains a lot," Clifton said, running his fingers across a large bump at the base of his skull. "Where are the others?" he asked, motioning toward the empty seats at the head table.

"They're in a chamber room, planning their next move," Dane

replied. "In fact, now that yer awake, we best be heading in to meet up with 'em."

"What about him?" Clifton pointed to Richard, surrounded by a number of young courtesans listening wide-eyed to his storytelling, vying for his attention.

Dane rolled his eyes. "That one's under a spell, he is. Enchanted by the young ladies surrounding him. A child and a fool!"

Richard looked over at Dane and replied, "If this is the reward for a child who is a fool," he motioned toward the girls, "then count me the greatest fool of them all."

The girls giggled and blushed, covering their faces with their fans.

"That's no problem at all," Dane said, standing and prancing behind the head table. "I already consider ya the greatest fool of them all."

Richard narrowed his eyes at Dane, now the only one smiling. "Come, Clifton. This way," Dane said. "We have work to do while the children stay here and play."

Richard pouted, crossing his arms over his chest, no longer enjoying the girls' attention. Clifton stood, grabbing a couple of pieces of bread and a handful of olives off the table. He met Dane before the large crimson backdrop hanging behind the head table. Dane pulled the curtain aside and ambled through. Clifton followed, passing beneath the stone archway and into a hall hidden by the curtain.

"This way, lad."

They moved quietly through the musty hall, the flaming sconces placed far from one another, and the wooden doors evenly spaced along both sides. The stones were cold, and water dripped off them. The laughter died as the guests moved farther and farther back, along with the playful strings of the quintet. Clifton imagined Richard still pouting at the table. He took a bite from his bread, chewed an olive, and placed the rest in his pocket for later. Dane stopped before a random door and stepped inside.

Chapter Twenty-Seven

Forces

A fire snapped and crackled the dry logs in the fireplace. Besides the sound of the quiet voices coming from around the corner, the room remained still. Every inch seemed covered with something, chairs draped with linens, portraits and oil paintings hanging on fifteen-foot tapestries, and antiques and statues situated throughout the room.

Clifton and Dane rounded the corner where Edward and Elizabeth sat at a large oak table. Henry leaned over parchments, pointing to a map while he spoke in low tones. Several large candles burned on and around the table. Clifton couldn't help but imagine all those brittle pages catching fire and burning up in an instant.

They looked up, and Edward stood. "Clifton, glad to see you are well."

Clifton forced a smile, rubbing the bump on his head. "Sorry about your foot."

"No apologies are necessary. However, I had never seen someone faint during a knighting ceremony before."

"I don't think it was the ceremony so much as it was the sword."

"Gentlemen, could we, please?" Henry motioned to the parchments and maps.

"Of course," Edward said. "Clifton, Dane, please. Take a seat." He directed them to their spots. "Continue, My Lord."

"At this time," Henry Tudor went on, "five thousand men in arms are ready and awaiting my arrival."

"That is all?" Elizabeth asked, her brow furrowed forward. "That will not be enough. My uncle has an army of ten thousand men trained for battle. We would be walking into a slaughter to take so few men to fight such an army."

Her conviction impressed Clifton. He had always thought medieval princesses to be delicate and beautiful, like porcelain dolls, and although Elizabeth was very beautiful, that was not who she was.

"We will be aided by the Stanley brothers," Henry said.

"Under whose command?" Edward asked.

"Thomas Stanley," Henry said, defensively, "who brings a force of six thousand men, making an army eleven thousand strong, more than enough to take on the king."

Edward mulled over the maps and parchments, though he didn't seem to be reading any of them. He met Henry's eyes. "And you trust him?"

Henry gathered his voice. "I trust him enough. And it does not matter, for we will battle with or without the Stanley brothers, though with them would bring more favorable odds."

Edward nodded in agreement and stood, pacing quietly. "And what of my uncle's forces? Who leads them?"

"Jasper has just received word from the Loyalist spies and should arrive shortly."

Clifton grabbed an olive from his pocket. The oil dripped from the smashed fruit, and he popped it into his mouth. There wasn't much for him to do, and the talk of war strategies was beyond him. He'd wished he'd grabbed more food before he left the banquet hall.

"What is the plan, Highness?" Dane asked, packing his pipe with fresh tobacco.

"That is up to Henry."

Henry turned to Dane. "The final plan has yet to be determined."

Uncertainty permeated the room. Edward undoubtedly felt it, too, and stood to speak. "I am certain, Henry, being unfamiliar with the land we plan to conquer and the arts in which to accomplish this great feat, your decision to employ other, stronger, more experienced men of battle was a most resourceful one. They lack your ability for planning and strategizing."

Henry nodded. "Thank you for your confidence, Edward."

"It is the truth, My Lord."

"So, who will you be employing to head up the Loyalist army?"

"John de Vere will be in charge of my army," Henry said. "Second in command will be Sir James Blount."

"Clifton, have you anything to add?" Edward asked.

Clifton stared up; three olives perched on his fingertips. He shook his head, his face growing hot as he gulped hard.

There was a light rap on the door. Jasper entered the room, locking arms with Henry at the elbows. Richard followed, still pouting, and took a seat in a padded chair near the fire. He didn't even look into the room where the others stood.

"My friend," Henry Tudor said. "Let us hope my spies have brought you valuable news."

"That they have," Jasper said. He bowed to Edward and nodded to Dane. "Welcome back, Sir Clifton. It is wonderful to see you well."

"Good to see you, too," Clifton said, shifting in his seat. The thick wood and sharp angles were taking a toll on his rump. What he wouldn't give for a Lazy Boy recliner.

"King Richard does indeed have an army ten thousand strong, according to your spies," Jasper said, leaning against the table. "However, most are not trained for battle as originally thought, mainly farmers and herdsmen, some blacksmiths and tradesmen, much the same as our numbers."

"You bring good tidings," Elizabeth said. "The king's soldiers will share our disadvantage on the battlefield."

"Indeed," Jasper continued. "The king has divided his army into three battles, assigning one to the Duke of Norfolk and another to the Earl of Northumberland. The majority of the army will remain under the experience of King Richard himself."

The air became stagnant and heavy. Finally, Edward cut through the silence. "So, uncle will lead on the battlefield." He smirked. "This could prove to be most promising."

The candle in the center dripped wax into a pool on the wooden table. Clifton found himself staring at it, drifting off into a daydream while the others continued their discussion of military tactics and who commanded what army. Clifton wanted to participate, wanted to ask questions, but he didn't understand half of what they were saying. And although he tried desperately to pay attention, he felt as if he were sitting through a lecture in Mrs. Kane's history class.

Clifton wondered if the party in the Great Hall had died down if those attending had even noticed the empty seats at the head table, the homecoming party missing. Probably not. With all the great food, music, and drinks, Clifton assumed the party had just gotten started when they'd left.

His thoughts drifted home to his parents, discovering an empty bedroom. His dad would be furious, especially after reading the fake apology letter he drafted to Ryan. Clifton wished he had erased it. His mom wouldn't be mad until after she found him safe and sound. Right now, she was probably too worried to be mad, calling every one of his friends and driving through neighborhood after neighborhood looking for him. And poor Pierce. He wouldn't understand any of it. He would simply miss his big brother and wonder when he would come home.

Clifton's eyelids grew heavy. He tried staying attentive, pretending to be looking along with the others at the maps and plans, but he couldn't. Richard had fallen asleep, curled up in the plush chair by the fireplace. His pout had changed to a smile in his sleep, and Clifton bet it was from all those soft cushions. Clifton assumed it would be considered rude to excuse himself to one of the chairs beside the fire, although his muscles twitched from fighting sleep.

He perched his elbows on the table and cupped his chin with his palms as his eyes closed and opened, in and out of sleep.

"The ship is prepared to sail across the English Channel...land at Mill Bay on the north side..." Henry said.

Clifton saw blackness. His eyes opened again.

"...men will be at the port to meet us," Henry said, tracing a path with his finger on the map.

Clifton's world again went black. But he still heard voices.

"...hope word has yet to reach my uncle..."

"...immobilize in Shrewsbury...decide best course from there..."

"...set sail tomorrow morning...."

With his elbows on the table, Clifton slid slowly, jolting up from his slipping hands. Finally, he gave in to sleep and stretched his arm out for a pillow. With his head down and his eyes closed, he heard Elizabeth say, "One thing is certain, in four weeks' time, King Richard III will be just a name in the history books."

Chapter Twenty-Eight
The Bell Turret

C lifton sprinted through an open field from Ryan, who was less than a hundred feet behind and gaining. The field dipped, and a large boulder grew closer. Clifton hurtled it, then crawled back to the boulder before Ryan reached the dip in the clearing. Leaning against cold stones, he braced for the worst.

In the silence, he stood to glance across the empty field. Ryan was nowhere. He turned, panicked, unsure which way to go if he should go anywhere at all. Suddenly, gravel dusted down onto his shoulders like light rain, and Clifton looked up. Ryan stood on top of the boulder, his hand raised, his axe's blunt edge reflecting the sunlight.

In the distance, someone called his name. Ryan let out a tribal scream then leapt through the air. Clifton shielded his head, shaking with fear, his whole body convulsing...

Clifton's eyes shot open. Richard leaned over him, shaking his shoulder. "Clifton, wake up!"

In the dark chamber room, Clifton couldn't tell the time, the heavy drapes blocking out the light. "What time is it?"

"It is four o'clock in the night. We must move quickly."

Clifton sat on the chair by the hearth. *What a bizarre dream.* He didn't remember dragging himself near the fireplace. Actually, the last thing he remembered was passing out on the table, which was now empty. Where was everyone? "What's the rush?"

"Uncle's spies have found us. We must set out for Harfleur at once." Richard flew out of sight.

Clifton shook his head, trying to wake up. He grabbed his boots and laced them; the leather warm from the fire's heat. He must have really knocked his head good because he couldn't remember taking them off.

Dane popped his head into the room. "Let's go, lad. Time is running out."

"Going as fast as I can," Clifton said, still half-asleep. He hurried to the door.

Richard stood in the hallway beside Edward and Elizabeth, who had traded her dainty dress for trousers and heavy boots. Henry led the group, with Jasper bringing up the rear.

"Let's move," Henry said.

They sped down the hall, their boots thumping the stone floor. Richard's sword scraped the wall the way nails scratch on a chalkboard. Clifton cringed as goosebumps raised his skin. Then suddenly, he stopped short.

"My sword," Clifton said. "I forgot it."

Henry turned sharply, his eyes glaring. "Go get it then." He shook his head and continued leading the group down the hall.

"I will go with the boy," Jasper said.

"Make haste," Henry called back.

Elizabeth squeezed Jasper's hand. "We will meet you at the chapel under the bell turret."

"Yes, My Lady," he said.

She released his hand and followed the others, disappearing around the corner and out of sight.

"Let's go," Jasper said, hurrying back down to the chamber room with Clifton trailing close behind.

Grabbing a small lantern from the mantel, Jasper lit the wick while Clifton searched for the sword. "It's not here," he said. He rushed into the other room, with the large table now cleared of maps and parchments, tripping on his own backpack in the darkness. His eyes slowly adjusted, and he made out his bow, quiver, and Excalibur leaning against the chair. Clifton gulped, remembering the weightiness of the sword, the world reflecting in the blade, lifting it with remarkable ease. He still couldn't wrap his brain around the sword's meaning, but this was not the time. Grabbing everything, he hurried into the other room.

"Found it," he hollered to Jasper.

"Hurry, then."

Clifton strapped the quiver across his chest and set down his backpack. What point would there be to carry it along? Something in his gut told him he'd better take it, so he threw it across his shoulders. He felt like a video game character, bow in one hand and Excalibur in the other.

"Here," Jasper said. "Use this."

He handed Clifton a sheath attached to a thick, leather belt. Clifton strapped it over the smaller belt holding his knife.

"Clifton, come on, please," pleaded Jasper, now standing in the hall.

They bolted back down the same corridor, rounded the corner, and halted in front of a small doorway. Jasper reached for the handle and stopped short.

"What's wrong?"

"It is scalding."

Clifton touched his fingertips to the door, yanking his hand away reflexively. "It's like it's on fire."

"It very well could be. Come, this way." Jasper backtracked down the corridor.

"Why was it so hot?" Clifton asked, jogging to keep up, his weapons slamming into one another like a cryptic one-man-band.

"I do not know with certainty. The last time I remember a door feeling that hot—" He looked quickly back over his shoulder at Clifton. "You will not be pleased to hear this, but it could possibly have been—a long-tailed crestback."

"A what?"

"A dragon."

Clifton's stomach tensed. His head tingled. "A dragon? That's impossible!"

"I know," Jasper said, following a split in the corridor to the left. "I have not seen any here since last summer."

The writings on the parchment in Flaxton Village jumped into Clifton's mind about Sir Edward the Lionheart. "No," he said, following closer behind Jasper. "I mean, it's impossible for a dragon to be here."

"Again, I know," Jasper said, following a downward slope in the curving passageway. "I thought they had all migrated to Sylvania."

Clifton stopped and adjusted his pack. "Oh," was all he managed to say.

"Hurry, Sir Clifton," Jasper said, his voice echoing through the winding corridor. "We are almost there."

Clifton swallowed hard. He wanted to cry. He wanted to scream. He desperately wanted to wake up from this dream. But it wasn't a dream. Because reality was never questioned in a dream, it was accepted. No matter how absurd or unbelievable it would be in waking life, it always made perfect sense in that place of dreams.

And this made no sense.

Jasper's shadow crossed the curve of the hall, a menacing monster moving downward until his lantern's light disappeared. In near darkness, Clifton sped to catch up. What else could he do? He was at the mercy of the moment, frozen in a past adventure.

Chapter Twenty-Nine

The Crestback

T he hall ended at a narrow shaft where a ladder led up to a round wooden door. After handing the lantern to Clifton, Jasper climbed the six rungs to the top, placed his ear against the wood, and listened. Clifton lifted the lantern to get a better look. Instead, he caught the light in his eyes, momentarily blinding himself, and for the next several minutes saw bright white spots each time he blinked.

"Hand me the lantern," Jasper said, reaching down.

"What did you hear?" Clifton asked, passing up the lantern.

"Nothing," Jasper answered. "But that does not mean much from down here." He pushed the door up slightly, then slowly lifted his head out through the opening bringing the lantern up and above him. "Follow me," he said, flinging the door wide and hurrying out the shaft.

Reaching the top, Clifton poked his head out and surveyed his surroundings; the cool air was a relief from the staleness of the shaft. They were on the far side of the Great Hall, past the chapel, in some alleyway in Èze. A few small fires burned in various places in the open field stretching between them and the chapel.

Jasper crossed, slinking in the building's shadows, using his robe to eclipse his lantern. Clifton's heart pounded in his chest as he nervously eyed the sky for any sign of a dragon.

They reached the end of a row of shops, and Jasper pointed ahead. "The chapel entrance is there, beyond that spruce tree. The others will be waiting in the bell turret." Looking up, he added, "The sky seems clear for the moment. If we run, we should reach the door in only a few moments. Hopefully, that will be enough time." He paused. "If only it were later in the morning."

"Why's that?" Clifton asked, unsure if he really wanted to know the answer.

"Crestback dragons are skilled hunters with keen night vision," Jasper whispered. "It is next to impossible to evade one once it has detected you. But they have trouble seeing in the daylight, especially in the moments of dusk and dawn when it is neither day nor night. They are almost blind, relying on their scent, which is poor."

"Why can't we wait till dawn?" Clifton asked.

"Because," Jasper said, "this breed of dragon can detect motion from very far away. Most likely, she is circling the area right now. We have no way of knowing."

"But she could have left, right?"

"Of course," Jasper said. "But we do not *know*. The dragon will find us if we wait too long. We either take our chances here or out there. The choice is yours, Sir Clifton. What would you have us do?"

Clifton looked up into the night sky. Dawn teased but would not come soon enough. Clouds covered the stars in patches, revealing the sky in jigsaw pieces. If only they could camouflage themselves somehow. Then, they could easily get across the field undetected. "That's it," Clifton said. "We can make a smoke covering."

"How will we do that?"

"Grab some hanging moss from over there," Clifton said, pointing to some trees.

Jasper went to retrieve the moss while Clifton broke twigs off a nearby bush, stealing looks in the sky for the crestback. He brought the kindling back into the shadow of the awning, opened the lantern to expose the flame, and set one of the sticks on fire. Jasper returned with an armful of moss and knelt beside Clifton.

"I need your cloak," Clifton said. "You won't get it back."

With a nod, Jasper removed his cloak, and the two laid it out flat, piling the branches and moss in its center. A loud swooshing near the chapel sent the hair on Clifton's neck straight up.

It could only be one thing.

He searched for the dragon, remembering the description of the bearded crocodilian with bat-like wings. After plunging the fiery stick into the ground, he ripped open his backpack and grabbed his three-ring binder. History, how appropriate. He tore out notebook pages, crumbled them into loose balls, and placed them around the moss and twigs.

"I hope this works," Clifton said, touching the lit stick to the paper. The dry summer left the wood brittle, and everything ignited quickly. Clifton took the last of his Dropwater, whispering a thank you to Liv, and poured it over part of the fire, extinguishing most of the flame. Billowing smoke rose up from the charred remains.

"Grab one side of the cloak," Clifton said. "I need you to help me drag it."

Jasper lifted one end and Clifton the other, folding the cloak like a taco leaving an opening in the center. Smoke caught in the wind. Small bits of wood smoldered, and the heat scorched Clifton's hands. He hoped the wood wouldn't burn through the cloak before they reached the chapel.

In an awkward relay race, they ran side by side, holding the cloak between them, trying to step in sync with one another through the darkness. Ash floated up from the opening, then fell as gentle black snow. From above, Clifton hoped they created a good enough covering to keep them off the crestback's radar.

Clifton hotfooted to the chapel door, and with no sign of the crestback by the halfway point, he whispered to Jasper, "I think we're gonna make it!"

A screech pierced the darkness, mimicking a bald eagle's cry.

The crestback's wings pressed through the clouds first, followed by a beast larger and more terrifying than the picture on the parchment had let on. Clifton held back his scream while the dragon passed directly overhead.

The dragon's spiny wings pushed out the air, waving the smoke covering away, leaving Jasper and Clifton completely exposed.

"She's turning around," Jasper yelled. "Run!"

Together, they dropped the cloak and sprinted across the field. Suddenly, Clifton remembered his dream. Was he dreaming of this moment, replacing Ryan for the crestback? He wished he knew how it would end. He didn't look back at Jasper. He didn't look up at the dragon. He just stared at the door, growing larger and larger the closer he came until, at last, he reached the knob and turned it. In horror, his hand stopped. The door was locked.

Chapter Thirty
No Way Out

"What do we do now?" Clifton asked, rattling the knob.

"Try not to die," Jasper said, pressing his back against the wood.

Changing direction, the crestback began her second run. She raised her red crest in defiance, the way a cat would when hissing. Vein-covered opaque wings stretched out well over fifteen feet from end to end.

Clifton remembered reading in the parchment how these dragons belched fire up to ten yards. She looked farther away than that, but had someone actually done the measurements? Clifton wasn't counting on it.

They were trapped, with nowhere to run. Every direction but

inside the chapel door meant revealing themselves out in the open, at the mercy of the crestback.

"What does she want? Is she hunting for food?" Clifton asked.

"Not likely," Jasper said.

"What then?" Clifton asked, the dragon now within fifty yards of the chapel.

"The crestback dragons migrate to Sylvania in the summer. Dragons in that region are usually captured by hunters," Jasper explained. "Some are studied, but many are killed and sold by the piece to magicians and sorcerers, or to certain merchants. The smartest are trained to be used as bounty hunters."

The dragon charged now only thirty-five yards from them. Clifton and Jasper pressed against the door.

"You think she's a bounty hunter?"

"She is not missing any pieces."

"For who, King Richard?"

"That is who I was considering," Jasper said. "She is here to capture, not kill."

Clifton gawked at Jasper's profile. He was not smiling.

The dragon soared, now twenty yards away and closing in fast. Clifton could almost see the reflection of the ground-fires bouncing off her shiny, black talons. When she ranged within fifteen yards, Clifton braced for the flames, squirming in anticipation for unimaginable heat. He burnt his hand in a campfire once. The burn shot pain through every nerve in his arm, and it throbbed for hours. And that was a small burn. He hoped Jasper was right about the dragon's purpose.

"Why would Richard go through all this trouble to capture his nephews if he only wants to kill them?" Clifton asked. The dragon was now just ten yards away.

"She is not here for them," Jasper said. "She's here for you. *You* hold the Arrow of Light."

Clifton's knees buckled. He thought he might faint. Why had he kept that awful arrow? It had brought him nothing but trouble. He should have left it in his closet and let Dane take it back.

The dragon hovered over the field, an immense six-hundred-pound beast with razor-sharp teeth and a spiked tail that whooshed through the air like a swinging club.

Jasper lifted his sword.

Clifton's eyes bugged. "You're going to fight her?" he asked.

"If I must," Jasper said. "At all costs, we must protect the arrow. I will fight her off as a distraction, and you must run to safety."

"What? I can't leave you." Clifton shook his head. "I can't run away like a coward."

"This is not about you, Clifton. You are the chosen one and must be protected. I have sworn my life to such."

The dragon screeched, and Clifton unsheathed his sword. "I won't leave you here to fight alone." He pointed the shaking tip of Excalibur up at the dragon in an *en garde* challenge.

Clifton didn't blink while the crestback hovered, flapping her large wings. She started gulping air and then took in a long, slow breath through her nostrils. Clifton hoped she wasn't preparing to breathe fire.

"She's preparing to breathe fire!" Jasper shouted.

There was no place to turn, nothing they could do, and neither of their swords would be a match for her flames — not even Excalibur.

"Brace yourself," Jasper said.

Clifton pressed his back hard against the door, not ready for the pain, thinking of all the things he hadn't done in his life. He wished he had kissed Pierce good-bye and told his dad he was sorry and his mom how much he loved her. He wished he had told Ava that he thought she was the most beautiful girl he had ever seen. But he hadn't. Now he never would. The dragon stretched her wings, filling every last space in her deep lungs. With closed eyes, Clifton braced for a spew of burning flame. But then the door behind him rattled, and he fell inward.

Chapter Thirty-One
Outwitted

lifton felt a hand grab the back of his collar and drag him far into the room, where he landed with a thud on the hard stone floor. The door slammed closed, but not before Clifton glimpsed the flame burning the grass and charring the dirt where he and Jasper had stood. They would have been toast.

"Now we are even," Edward said, helping him to his feet.

Clifton smiled. "I sure am glad to see you."

"She nearly scorched us," Jasper said.

"I thought you said she was here to capture, not kill?" Clifton asked, sheathing his sword into the scabbard around his waist.

"Apparently, I misspoke," Jasper said, sheathing his own sword.

"She will be back," Edward said. "Before she returns, we need to get to the bell turret to meet the others."

Edward led them through the dark twisting and turning halls until they reached the winding stairwell at the base of the turret platform. They climbed the stairwell that was so narrow Clifton could only see the next step as he peered through the open squares spaced between the tower blocks. The crestback patrolled the air, screeching as her nostrils snorted spurts of black smoke. Quickening his step, Clifton pushed into Jasper's rear-end.

"Speed it up, man," Clifton said. "She's gonna cook us in here."

"Going as fast as I can, Sir Clifton," he replied.

"We have almost reached the top," Edward said.

Clifton wiped sweat from his brow, glancing through each open square until he reached the platform, where the others stood waiting.

"Hurry, Jasper," Elizabeth said. "We're running out of time."

A circle, etched into the stone, covered most of the belfry's floor, the radius several feet out from the bell itself — a white powder filled in the etched line. Henry Tudor leaned against the far wall, holding the bell's rope in his hands. Elizabeth grabbed Edward and Richard, pulling them close to her within the perimeter of the circle.

"Stop standing like a stone, lad," Dane said, yanking Clifton by the arm. "Get inside the circle. Unless ya want to stay here with her." He pointed outside to the crestback hovering near the open bell turret.

What was everyone doing? Did no one understand the predicament they were in, standing inside some strange circle like sitting ducks? With one blow, she could crisp them like ducks. "Are you ready, Jasper?" Henry asked.

"Almost," Jasper replied, pulling a small black pouch off his belt.

"We are not going to make it," Elizabeth said, squeezing the princes tighter against her sides.

"What's happening?" Clifton asked. He stepped away from the crestback, moving toward the stairs to escape.

"Shut up, lad," Dane yelled, thrusting him back into the circumference of the circle. "Don't move!"

"Now, Jasper?" Henry asked.

"Now."

Henry jerked the rope, and the bell clamored through the still night air. The crestback roared, shaken by the noise. Jasper ambled through the circle, chanting in low tones, sprinkling a sandy substance from his pouch over each of their heads and shoulders. The bell pealed louder.

The crestback appeared agitated, flapping her black wings, shaking her head, slamming her club tail in the air, shrieking and wailing. Clifton covered his ears. After a while, the crestback shifted into an offensive stance, taking in a slow, long breath, her black eyes staring at her targets in the bell turret.

"She's about to blow," Clifton shouted.

"How much longer?" Elizabeth asked.

Jasper methodically sprinkled the sandy substance over the area and beneath the pealing bell, chanting gibberish like a monk. Henry released the rope and lurched inside the apparent safety of the circle, the power of the bell's peal diminishing. "Any second now," he said, placing his arm around Elizabeth and the princes.

With both arms raised, Jasper chanted vociferously from his place near the bell, until he uttered the last of his undecipherable words. The floor of the tower shook. The crestback released her morbid flame. Clifton winced, covering his head and crouching to the stone floor. The sand lifted around him and hung, suspended in midair. The room quaked. The dragon's fire reached the tower walls. Clifton closed his eyes and screamed, his voice shrill and piercing.

Everything burst and muffled as if underwater. Clifton's skin singed from the crestback's flame, then instantly cooled, his flesh pulsed in pins and needles, from head to toe. He forced his eyes open, finding himself enveloped in darkness. No ground beneath his feet. No image of the bell turret, his companions, or the crestback. At least she was gone. He had a slight awareness of motion through a breeze in his hair and the rushing of his stomach. But he couldn't tell what direction he moved if any.

Maybe I'm dead.

Clifton passed through various pressure points, squeezing in from the sides, seeming to press the air from his lungs. Then he was pushed down, mashing his head into his feet, or so it felt. Wind blasted at him from different directions, perpetually changing, and he closed his eyes from the pressure. He heard nothing when he screamed until with a snap, everything abruptly stopped.

Chapter Thirty-Two
Set Sail

C lifton hesitated to move, to breathe, to open his eyes. A noise like a slapping hand smacked his ears. Was it water? Perhaps the lapping of the Mediterranean Sea against the shore. A smell drifted to his nose. Was it sulfur? Maybe what the dragon used to create fire in her glands. But on second thought, it smelled more like salt. And the shrieking of the dragon had vanished, replaced by the screeching of birds.

He uncovered his head and opened his eyes, squinting in sudden daylight. Seagulls flew overhead. Water lapped against the wharf. But he no longer saw the Mediterranean or the bell turret. He saw no landmarks from Èze. Instead, he stood on the deck of a large ship.

"Don't move too quickly, lad," Dane warned. "Takes a few moments to adjust to the changes."

"Where's the crestback?"

"She's long gone," Dane said, carrying a rope across the deck. "Probably looking for us and going mad."

Clifton wiped the dust off his hands and took a step toward the edge of the ship. His knees wobbled. "How is this possible?"

"Jasper spent some time in the far east," Dane said, wrapping the rope around his arm into a heap. "Let's just say he learned some very interesting tricks from his journeys there."

"Including evading dragons," Elizabeth said.

Clifton turned. The sun shimmered in her hair, and he couldn't help but notice how beautiful she was, even dressed in burlap pants and hide boots.

"How are you, Clifton?" she asked.

"I'm not sure yet."

Men scurried around the ship, wearing plain breeches and doublets, carrying supplies, tightening ropes, and bringing up the sails.

Clifton scanned the deck. "Where's Edward?"

"In the Captain's Quarters reviewing the maps with Henry," Richard said. "We should be set to sail at any moment."

Clifton turned back to the edge of the ship. A small, seaside wharf, lined with wooded shops, stretched out over the dingy dock, not the breathtaking view from Èze's mountains.

"Where are we?" Clifton asked.

"On the English Channel," a gruff sailor answered in passing.

Clifton jumped. The sailor laughed. "Didn't mean to startle you. The name's Alfred Mansfield."

"Clifton Chase."

"You ever sail before, Clifton?"

He shrugged. "Once or twice. But not on a ship like this."

"Aye, and you never will again," Alfred said. "First rule of sailing. Many hands make a light load."

Alfred threw a thick rope at Clifton. It was attached to something so heavy that it pulled Clifton up against the side of the ship with a crack. Dane jumped up and grabbed Clifton by the waist. Elizabeth covered her mouth and gasped.

"Good work, dwarf," Alfred said. His smile exposed yellowing teeth and empty spaces like vacant windows. He bowed. "Welcome aboard." He limped away cackling while Clifton and Dane held tight to the rope attached to the heavy anchor.

"I hate sailors," Dane said. "Dirty, nasty creatures."

Dane and Clifton heaved on the rope, pulling the anchor up to the side of the ship before securing it to the stern cleat. Edward walked toward them. "Well-done, friends. Way to jump in and give a hand."

Dane grunted, swore, and crossed to the opposite side of the ship. "Is he all right?" Edward asked.

"Yeah," Clifton said. "He's fine."

"Very well," Edward continued. "Glad to see we are in high spirits. We set sail immediately for Milford Haven." He motioned up toward the clear sky. "Should only take us a week with fair weather such as this. I hope you are up for a sail, Clifton."

"At this point, I'm up for anything."

Elizabeth grinned and grabbed Clifton's hand. "So our adventure has begun, and God willing, it will be over quickly, and He will keep us all safe."

"And keep the seas safe," Richard added, rubbing his stomach.

"Clifton, you are brave to have taken this willingly upon yourself. I cannot imagine how to repay you for your sacrifice."

Clifton squinted. "I'm not sure I'm following what you mean, My Lady."

"Our adventure to England will be dangerous, but you have proven yourself worthy and true. I am certain you will not let us down in the next chapter to come." She dropped his hand and stepped toward the Captain's Quarters.

"Excuse me, My Lady?" Clifton asked. Elizabeth turned to face him. "What exactly will we be doing once we get to England?"

Her eyes narrowed, and her cheeks lost their dimples. With a fiery bite, she said, "We will find my uncle. And when we do, you are going to kill him."

"Me? Why me?"

She looked at him, confused. "It has always been that way

throughout history. Everyone the Arrow of Light chooses must face the path they were chosen for."

"And you think I was chosen to kill your uncle?"

She laughed. "Of course. If not that, then for what?"

Clifton gulped hard. He didn't watch her leave. He felt nauseated as he slipped down the side of the ship onto a large crate and closed his eyes. All he could see was the oil painting of the boy with the arrow; the face morphed closer to his own. But this time, the ground around him was stained crimson with blood.

Chapter Thirty-Three
Missing

After three days of sailing, Clifton's stomach finally reached balance with the English Channel. He sat on an empty crate, relaxing with his friends beneath a red sunset. Dane smoked his slender pipe, his hairy feet resting on a sack of supplies while Elizabeth and Richard played dice. Edward and Henry had retreated to the Captain's Quarters, presumably charting courses and planning the route they would take once they reached Milford Haven.

Clifton's eyes grew heavy, his potato soup and stale bread digesting. He stood to stretch and stared across the channel. Nearing the halfway point of their journey, the wharf was long gone, and Milford Haven's seaport not yet close enough, Clifton noticed only small islands here and there jutting out like obstacles in a pinball machine. The murky water grew dark and ominous, the cold air warning of icy seas. Clifton's gaze locked on the channel while lulling voices rose from the depths, faint songs that mesmerized, seeming to call his name.

"Don't want to fall in there," Dane said.

Clifton turned. "Why? Because the water's cold?"

"Sea serpents," Dane responded, through a cloud of scented smoke.

Clifton laughed. "Sea serpents? You can't be serious."

Dane stared; his brow furrowed. "I am most serious. Not to mention whatever other foul creatures lurk in the depths of these waters."

Clifton shivered, the voices resonating from the sea, echoing in his ears. "What do you mean?"

"Just fables, Clifton," Elizabeth said. "Bedtime stories told to scare children and give dwarves something to talk about."

"Suit yerselves," Dane said, returning his attention to his pipe. "But don't say ya weren't warned."

Clifton was about to ask more about the creatures when the hinged door off the main deck opened. Edward, Jasper, and Henry exited, crossing the deck to join the others.

"Clifton," Edward said. "Gather your things from below and bring them up."

"Sure," Clifton said. "Is everything okay?"

"Yes," Henry responded. "We only need the Arrow of Light."

Clifton crossed the deck, looking back once over his shoulder, catching Henry exchanging words with Elizabeth. Her face painted with shock, perhaps terror, he couldn't tell. Clifton squirmed. He passed several sailors before he reached the aft door, and they followed him with their eyes while Clifton passed through, closing the door tightly behind him.

Something wasn't right.

Clifton climbed the ladder below deck, rocking through the narrow hall to his quarters. His room was small, containing a hard bed and a desk. With the sun's last light spreading weakly through the circular window, Clifton lit the lantern on the table. His backpack lay open, his things tossed across his bed. He had wedged his pack deep beneath the mattress, like Dane had told him to, covering it with an empty burlap sack from the kitchen. Someone had been in his room.

The Arrow of Light was missing.

Chapter Thirty-Four

Traitor

"**I**t's gone," Clifton panted, after sprinting to the deck.

"What do you mean it is gone?" Edward asked. "How is that possible?"

"We are the only ones who knew," Henry said.

"Who could have taken it?" Richard asked, his eyes pinched in worry.

"I don't know," Clifton said. "I hid it under my bed like I was supposed to, but when I got in my room, my pack was on my bed, and all my stuff was thrown across the blanket."

"Someone has betrayed us," Henry said. "A traitor among us." He scanned the faces of the others, his ears reddening, his pupils dilating.

"No, My Lord," Edward said. "Not among *us*. The only traitor is the king of England, and he has many spies to carry out his business."

"Because he is too much of a coward to do it himself," Richard said, his tone rising.

Edward held him by the shoulders; the brothers stood face to face. "Yes, he is a coward. But you will do no good to fight him from this ship. Save your conviction for the battlefield." He kissed Richard's forehead and released him. "Right now, we have more pressing matters at hand. We must find the arrow."

They assembled the crew on the deck, a motley bunch of sweaty men in mismatched, layered garments smelling of the briny seas. Edward stood on the upper deck with his brother, sister, and Henry behind him.

"Men," Edward said. "You have been chosen to this crew for your loyalty to my father, Edward IV, King of England."

A bald man with a trim mustache near the front of the crowd hollered in agreement.

"We are but days away from port where we will meet with other Loyalists to attack our common enemy, a traitor who has stolen our land and proclaimed himself king."

Many of the men grunted or booed, pumping their fisted hands into the air.

"King Richard has many spies in his service," Edward continued. "And among us, dear brothers, a traitor stands."

With gasps and foul language, the crew shouted their disgust, each man eyeing the one next to him.

"Our new friend, Sir Clifton Chase of Melbourne, has been chosen to aid us on our quest."

Sailors whispered, looking around for Clifton, who had stepped far back into the crowd, casting his eyes to the deck.

A broad-shouldered man with a lazy eye surrounded by a jagged yellow scar yelled, "Perhaps he's the traitor!"

The crowd grew rambunctious, grinding their teeth, stomping their boots, while the witch hunt became more powerful. Several sailors hollered their agreement of this theory, like gas to a burning flame, igniting paranoia. Clifton sank into the background, his fight or flight kicked in, but he had nowhere to run. If Edward didn't get this crowd under control, Clifton would be at the mercy of a riot. And probably find himself at the bottom of the channel.

"Enough!" Edward commanded; his arms lifted to regain the seamen's attention. "Hear me, for, upon my honor, he is no traitor."

"Then have him show his face if he's got nothing to hide," shouted a man with long, black hair braided in a knot down his back.

"Very well," Edward said. "If it will appease you."

Dane nudged Clifton in the side. Clifton shook his head furiously. Dane nudged him again, harder this time. "Go, lad, if ya value yer life at all."

"Clifton, please step forward," Edward said, searching the crowd for his friend.

With a heavy sigh, Clifton lifted his eyes and slowly worked his way to the front of the crowd, squeezing through the swarming hornet's nest of men. When he reached the upper deck, he turned to face the crowd.

"This boy?" the bald sailor asked. "He looks too tidy to fight."

"Yeah, look how clean his fingernails be," cackled a man with a large wart on his nose — a wildfire of sneers and raucous laughter spread through the crowd.

"He carries the Arrow of Light," Edward shouted.

The sailors quieted. Their banter and laughter halted in waves. Each seaman stared differently at Clifton, the pauper who became a prince, the boy who became a hero. Clifton grew self-conscious, forcing himself to stand tall though his foot tapped the deck nervously.

"The arrow chose him," Edward continued. "So, you will serve him, as you would serve me."

One by one, the sailors took a knee. Clifton peered up at Edward, who smiled down at him. Clifton smiled back a half-hearted grin.

Henry stepped forward. "But one of you already knew he carried the arrow," he said. "For the Arrow of Light has been taken by one of you."

The men got to their feet, grumbling over the atrocity.

"It will soon be discovered who has committed this heinous

crime, and that man will walk the plank to his sure death," Edward said. "Dwarf, examine each man's quarters. Leave no space unchecked."

Dane nodded and left the deck, followed by Jasper, who silently slipped from behind the princes and down the steps to aid Dane in the search.

Edward continued to speak to the sailors, and Clifton surveyed their faces. Something wasn't right, like a splinter in his brain he couldn't reach. After days together, Clifton recognized most of the sailors from seeing them mull about on the ship, although he knew only a handful by name. And scanning them all together in one spot, he realized what was the matter.

One of them was missing.

Chapter Thirty-Five
Alfred Mansfield

C lifton snuck across the deck while the sailors, engrossed with the prince's words, violently accused one another. No one questioned what he was doing. Stealthily, he approached the wooden door leading down to the belly of the boat and reached for the knob. It turned, opening from the inside, as Dane and Jasper exited.

"Hello, lad," Dane said. "No luck yet, but we're still…"

"I know who has it," Clifton interrupted.

Jasper huddled them off to the side near tarp-covered cargo stacked against the wooden railing. "Who?"

"His name is Alfred Mansfield. He nearly knocked me overboard with the anchor my first day here. Remember, Dane? You had to grab me to keep me from flying off the ship."

"Do I ever," Dane growled. "Didn't like that man from the

moment he opened his trap."

"Me neither," Clifton said. "And he's the only sailor that I don't see around. Anywhere. I've pretty much accounted for everyone else, at least the best I can. But I know he's missing. And I have a feeling he's trouble."

"We've thoroughly searched the sleeping quarters," Jasper said. "They are empty."

"We have to tell Edward," Clifton said. "I bet anything if we find Alfred, we find the arrow."

"Wait here," Jasper said. "I will go inform the prince." He bowed slightly and skirted away.

The sailor's anger had died down, the fighting ceased. Edward had regained control and prevented a mutiny. Things were still bad, with the arrow and Alfred missing, but at least Clifton didn't have to worry about being thrown into the sea anymore. Water tapped against the wooden planks of the hull, the peaceful waves, and clouds in exact opposition to the commotion on deck.

"Ain't nothing like being out to sea, eh, boy?" Dane said.

He didn't answer, and they stood in silence.

Clifton pressed to the edge of the handrail and peered down. It wasn't a long distance, maybe a hair over thirty feet to the cold, murky waters. Soft singing wafted up from the deep. Clifton side-glanced Dane. He didn't seem to hear it. Clifton watched the water, leaning farther over the handrail, as the singing intensified.

If he could only get closer…

A dark image darted below the surface. Then another. Were they dolphins? They might have been if they were sailing in Florida, but this was the English Channel. Maybe they were porpoises. They'd been known to swim in these cold waters. The images propelled underwater, pacing beneath him. His chest pressed against the bough, his feet barely touching the deck.

Just a little closer….

He strained his eyes, thinking he could make out what kinds of creatures swam below the surface, their hypnotic singing growing louder. He leaned farther still, his feet now off the deck, teetering his weight on his mid-section, the singing clearer…

Dane yanked Clifton back and spun him around. "What in the name of God were ya doing, boy?"

For a moment, Clifton couldn't remember why he needed yanking.

The others had arrived.

"Going for a swim, were you?" Elizabeth asked with a dimpled smile.

"No, I—uh," Clifton stuttered. "I thought I saw something." He pushed his hair off his face.

"Clifton, Jasper told me of your suspicions," Edward said. "Who is this sailor Alfred of whom you speak?"

"Just some guy I met at port, if you could call that a meeting."

"And what of his appearance?"

Clifton shrugged. "I don't know. He was missing some teeth."

Dane laughed. "Might as well tell us he had a face, boy. Would be about as much help with this brood of men."

"You saw him, too, Dane. Help me out here."

Dane tensed. "I saw only his backside. I was too busy diving past him to save yer life before ya toppled overboard."

"Gentlemen, please," Edward said. "This is not helping."

Dane grunted and looked away. Clifton continued. "He was tall, maybe six feet. Dark eyes and hair to about his shoulders, maybe close to your age, Henry."

"Anything more?" Edward asked, implying Clifton's description was far from helpful.

Clifton shrugged. "Nothing comes to mind."

The group stood in silence. Clifton thought hard for something that could actually be helpful. His eyes popped. "You know, come to think of it, I haven't seen him very much since we left port, maybe once or twice. That's kind of odd, isn't it? It's like he's been hiding."

Edward and Richard shared a thought with their glances.

"Brother," Edward said. "When we were children and would sail with father, do you remember what you would do when it was time for schooling?"

Richard laughed. "Of course. I would hide away so that I would not have to do lessons."

"That's right." Edward faced Elizabeth. "Sister, do you remember where we would find our dear brother when he so cleverly hid away?"

"Yes, Edward, I do." Elizabeth smiled and pointed. "Up there. In the crow's nest."

Chapter Thirty-Six
Crow's Nest

The group of men descended angrily to the base of the mast, fists raised, voices shouting, and swearing so badly that Clifton almost covered his own ears. He finally understood where the expression 'swears like a sailor' came from.

Henry rushed to the front of the crowd beneath the crow's nest. His stern face pulled forward in anger, and he lifted his head. "Alfred Mansfield!"

The mob fell silent.

"Alfred Mansfield, show yourself!"

Nothing stirred in the crow's nest.

"Traitor! Coward!" Edward said. "You will return what you have stolen at once and face a sure death by walking the plank."

Clifton shivered, thinking about the figures darting beneath the surface. He couldn't explain it, but he didn't think they were friendly.

A hoarse voice drifted down. "I will do no such thing."

"What is he thinking?" Clifton whispered to Dane. "He's on a ship in the middle of the English Channel, surrounded. He's got no chance."

Dane shook his head. "He's got the arrow, lad. Ya still don't understand? The power is in his hands if he's not too much of a fool to figure it out."

A cold chill crossed Clifton's skin. In the distance, the soft voices chimed again, their song familiar in the way a scent can trigger a memory. Unexplainably, he felt a strong pull toward the water and fought the urge to run to the edge of the ship and dive in.

Jasper crossed the deck to the base of the crow's nest; his head wound tightly inside an ornate cloth. A new black robe, decorated with symbols in gold and silver threads, skimmed the deck. In his hand, he held a sword, the hilt shaped into a figure Clifton couldn't make out from a distance. The men whispered, a wave of terror sweeping through the air.

"What is that on the hilt?" Clifton asked.

"It's an eight-headed serpent," Richard said. "That's the sword of Kusanagi."

"The sword of who?"

Richard turned wide-eyed. "You do not know the lore?"

Clifton shook his head.

"Quiet!" Dane snapped. "Listen closely."

Richard leaned in under Clifton's nose, a childish grin on his face. "Kusanagi is the Japanese god of storms who slay an eight-headed dragon with that sword, the Sword of the Gathering Clouds of Heaven."

"Pipe down," Dane said, through gritted teeth.

"The sword was used to direct the wind as an assault upon Kusanagi's enemies."

"And Jasper has it?"

Richard nodded, his eyebrows arched and raised as if preparing to jump off his face. "Jasper is a man of much mystery. You can never be surprised by anything he does."

Jasper chanted in the same language he used to evade the crestback back in Èze. His arms slowly lifted, raising the sword above his head. His palms pressed together with the blade between them; the eight-headed dragon pointed skyward. Kusanagi's sword illuminated, sending blinding light through the air.

"Oh, no," Dane said.

"What?" Clifton asked. "What's happening?"

"I can't be certain," Dane said, taking slow strides backward. "But I think I've heard this one before."

"What does that mean?"

"It means, ya'd best find something nailed down. And hold on tight." Dane disappeared through the crowd.

Dark clouds rolled in from thin air. Thunder clapped and lightening flashed. The sailors dissipated to man their positions, heaving sails, tightening ropes, and shouting commands. Jasper chanted louder, his voice growing in harmony with the howling winds and threatening storm. Then his eyes glazed over in a milky-white film. He had fallen into a trance, the conjurer of the storm.

Clifton dodged the wind, searching for something to brace against. The rocking ship knocked him off-balance as he strained to keep his footing. Large waves crashed against the hull and spilled over the sides drenching the deck. In desperation, Clifton grabbed hold of a heavy rope anchored to the sidewall and held on for his life. Pandemonium swelled, the rushing sailors hollered, fighting with the slick deck to stay grounded. Rain poured down in heavy streams and the ship quaked, rocking in sharp angles, the crow's nest bent like a palm tree in a hurricane.

Jasper was trying to shake Alfred out.

The idea was brilliant, really.

Tethered against the rope, Clifton braced, squinting against the stinging rain, shoving toward the base of the mast. He had almost made it when the boat dropped so deep Clifton panicked, thinking it would capsize.

Through the darkness, a light glowed, not from the Sword of the Gathering Clouds of Heaven, but from something else. The diamond tip of the Arrow of Light poked through the center of the coiled pile of thick rope Clifton held to stay onboard. It swayed, a snake dancing for a charmer, the shaft brilliant against the black clouds and rain.

Clifton pulled harder and lunged toward the arrow when he was close enough. A massive wave struck the hull. Lightning cracked the mast, snapping off the crow's nest, sending it toppling to the deck with a hard crash. Clifton grabbed the arrow with one hand; his other hand cramped around the slick, knotted fibers of the rope.

The ship shifted, and his grip slipped off the rope, knocking him to the deck, his head smacking against the wood. He saw stars. The ship corrected, rolling too far in the opposite direction, shuffling Clifton like an air hockey puck to the opposite edge where he rolled over the wooden handrail and plunged on his back into the channel. Lighting flashed, revealing to Clifton that Alfred Mansfield had also tumbled over the handrail.

And was headed straight for him.

Chapter Thirty-Seven
Overboard

C lifton slammed the channel's surface, the water so cold it snatched his breath away. His muscles became rigid as he plunged deeper, the arrow clenched in his fist. He twisted to face what he hoped was up, but the sea and clouds soaked up the light like a black hole. He forced his legs to kick, his arms to tread, as he swam for the top before his burning lungs gave way. In a final burst, he broke through the channel's skin, gulping hungry breaths. He blinked through the rain. Where was Alfred?

Two large hands pressed on his shoulders from behind, shoving Clifton underwater before he could take in a breath. He squirmed away and kicked off to the side. Clifton shot back up to the surface. Alfred waded a few feet away.

"Give me that back," Alfred yelled, lurching at the arrow and grabbing Clifton by the wrist. He was much stronger than Clifton, whose wrist ached from twisting and bending.

With his free hand, Clifton swung at Alfred's head, punching him over and over again. Alfred released his grip with a yelp. Clifton kicked off the man's gut and swam far away.

Clifton looked up to the ship. Many of the sailors leaned over the railing watching. Elizabeth's face streamed with tears, and Dane shouted, pointing into the distance. Although the storm was dying down, Clifton couldn't understand him.

What was he pointing at?

Clifton scanned the sea. Two scaly islands rolled in and out of the channel, seemingly disconnected. They went under. Something slimy brushed his leg. Clifton kicked, hoping it wasn't one of the sea serpents Dane had talked about.

What was he supposed to do?

He could never out swim one, let alone get away from Alfred first. Then, Clifton remembered the figures he had seen earlier, the ones singing so beautifully. Maybe they were the scaly humps he had seen. He hoped.

Alfred didn't seem to notice or care what those humps were either way. "You'll pay for that," Alfred screamed over the storm, then dove into the waves.

Clifton swam hard for the ship until Alfred yanked his leg and pulled him under again. He opened his eyes. The salt burned briefly, and the murky water clouded everything outside of an arm's length. Alfred clamped Clifton's leg, pulling him closer, wrestling for possession of the arrow. Something massive swam past them with a shriek. The look on Alfred's face spread terror through Clifton's blood. He used the fraction of a second to fight the man off, but Alfred quickly recovered, his hand like a vice grip pinching Clifton's flesh.

Clifton didn't know how much longer he could hold on. The water was too cold, and his muscles were failing. Then he remembered something Dane said about the arrow. He could almost hear his voice:

"Attaches itself to its chosen possessor...passes on protection and wisdom."

Of course. He held the Arrow of Light. An insurance policy guaranteeing long life, protection, and wisdom. If he only knew how it worked. He clenched his fist tightly around the shaft, wondering how to unlock its power. Alfred wrapped his hands around Clifton's neck, pressing on his windpipe. Clifton concentrated on the arrow, begging it to help him. His throat burned; his mind muddled as Alfred pressed harder.

"Please, help me," Clifton thought, pleading with the arrow to come to life.

Clifton's eyes rolled back. The shaft did not glow. Even in the current, the Simurgh feathers looked still as wood. He was going to die in 1485. What a paradox.

The water around them shuddered as great waves rippled and swirled. The sea serpent. If he could twist around, he might be able to use Alfred as a buffer. Maybe even bait. With much effort, Clifton kicked his legs to maneuver them around. Humps in the water grew closer, off Alfred's right shoulder, and with a jerk, Alfred's hands were ripped away as his body was dragged off. All that was left of the man was his scream in a trail of lingering bubbles.

The shock waves continued, and Clifton tumbled, as he had many times in the surf on Melbourne Beach. The long tail of the sea serpent appeared in front of him swishing like a humongous eel in the water. It turned around immediately as if folding in half. It was coming back for Clifton. Its many heads faced him staring with mouths gaping, mouths that had devoured Alfred. He didn't count the number of heads as he tumbled, but he would have bet there were eight.

With all the faith he could find, he begged the arrow to help him. He challenged its power, trying to believe its purpose for choosing Clifton was for something far greater than this creature's dinner.

Within reach of the monster's jagged teeth, Clifton screamed, releasing his last air reserves. If he were going to die here, he'd rather drown than be eaten. The serpent's eight jaws hinged open, the suctioning water pulling Clifton in with it. The mouths were like vast caverns of black oil. This was it. The end. Then, something grabbed him from behind. Whatever it was, it pulled him out of the vortex at an unbelievable speed.

The monster closed its jaws and faded into the blackness. Clifton sped backward, desperate for air. Moving farther away from the monster, the ship, his friends, and consciousness, deep down into the black sea.

Chapter Thirty-Eight
Rescued

Clifton was seconds away from passing out when a slender hand secured a gelatinous device to his face. It shrank to fit, suctioning to his forehead, cheeks, and chin, and he could see through it, the material resembling a jellyfish. More importantly, the jellyfish mask allowed him to breathe.

As he caught his breath, he wondered who was pulling him and where they were taking him. The slender hand could never be attached to something so hideous as the sea serpent. He remembered the figures he had seen earlier, swimming below the ship's deck before all the chaos with the storm and Alfred. It had to be one of those creatures who had rescued him from those eight hungry mouths. Maybe they were friendly after all.

Resonating through the black waters, a clear melody of a hundred voices sang out. Clifton thought of his mother tucking him into bed at night when he was little. And of Pierce when he caught a fit of giggles. And of his father during their trips alone fishing, when they talked until the sun set.

Slowly, light filtered through from somewhere beneath him. Clifton tried to turn his body to look below but couldn't. His captor's grip held too strong.

"Be still, Clifton Chase," a strange voice sang in his head.

As they swam, the light intensified, and Clifton glimpsed a seaweed forest. Tall mountains surrounded them as they passed through a canyon covered in beautifully colored corals and swaying sea plants in bloom. The landscape was enchanting, and without the water, Clifton thought the view would be the same here as his pass through the forests and mountains of England.

The tops of large structures appeared, jutting up like stalagmites through the dense seaweed forest. Clifton was taken lower, through the seaweed beds, and he couldn't see for a moment, as when descending in an airplane through clouds.

When the forest cleared, Clifton gasped. He swam over an ancient city. Massive coral pillars lined the open streets where schools of fish swam freely, and seahorses pulled chariots. Square buildings, resembling ancient Roman architecture, bordered the open design of the cityscape.

Closer still, he could make out the details of a paved shell road intersecting the city's center, leading to the steps of a palace. Clifton couldn't believe his eyes. And even more impressive than the underwater city were its inhabitants. Swimming in the water and riding on the seahorse-drawn chariots, and most assuredly the species of the creature pulling Clifton from behind were unmistakably mermaids.

Chapter Thirty-Nine

Another King

T he mermaids lowered Clifton to the seafloor and released
him. A crowd of merpeople had gathered, no longer singing.
On his left, a chiseled merman stood at attention. On his
right, a brown-skinned mermaid floated, her green hair fanning like
seaweed. His kidnappers or his saviors? Clifton tightened his grasp
on the Arrow of Light.

The palace's coral doors swung open, displacing sea creatures
that had settled into crevices. A short, chubby merman swam out
wearing a crown of conch shells and starfish.

"Welcome, Clifton Chase of the other world. Welcome to
Cantre'r Gwaelod." He raised his arms and circled them around.

"Welcome," the merpeople chorused.

Clifton smiled, and the jellyfish device squirmed to stay in place.

"This is truly an honor. An honor indeed, you see. You are quite the celebrity in this kingdom." The pudgy merman winked.

"Thank you, Sir."

"Highness," the green-haired mermaid corrected.

"Oh, Highness," Clifton said.

"I am King Gwyddno Garanhir, king of the Merpeople, and not a bad looking king, I might add. Cha-kha!" He guffawed at himself. "Now, where was I? Oh, yes. I am King Gwyddno Ga—"

"You mentioned that already, Highness," said the merman.

King Gyddno paused, stared at the merman with a look that could have passed for rage, then simply smiled, and said, "Indeed, I did. Thank you, Ashpenaz. Now that it is established as to who I am, I will adjourn this meeting with a farewell to my subjects." He nodded to the crowd with a dismissive wave, and the merpeople disbursed.

"My finest guards," he said to the two mers next to Clifton. "Thank you for a job well-done. You may leave me with my guest."

The two mers obeyed the king's command; only, they didn't stray very far.

King Gwyddno scooted to Clifton, his round belly preceding the rest of him. "My, this is a treat, you see?" King Gwyddno said, placing an arm around Clifton to anchor him to the seafloor. "Are you well, my lad? Mer-travel can be heavy on the stomach, though it's light on the feet, you see?"

"Yes, Highness. I feel fine."

"Superb. And how are things at the surface level?"

"Uh, okay...I guess."

"Hhmm? Well, I suppose you're right. Conversations should be deeper than how things are on the surface level. Cha-kha!" He snorted, chuckling at his own joke. "Now then, won't you honor me with your presence at a feast I will hold to honor you?"

"Seems I don't have much of a choice, Highness. Considering the circumstances."

"Don't weigh me down with logic, my lad. Too much buoyancy for that. Simply say yes."

"Okay, then. Yes."

"Splendid!" The king linked arms with Clifton, and they moved awkwardly away from the palace. King Gwyddno strode along the paved road as Clifton bobbed in the water. On a hillside seabed, dozens of merservants set tables and chairs made from oversized clam shells.

"Do you see that table over there, my lad?" King Gwyddno said. "It once belonged to a great Viking vessel. The shipwreck was a most delightful find, most delightful indeed."

"Are all of your tables made from shipwrecks?"

King Gwyddno stopped, staring up at Clifton. "Why yes, they are. What a smart boy. Very, very smart."

They kept moving, and Clifton touched the jellyfish-like apparatus attached to his face. It was solid, yet squishy, pulsing in rhythm to his breathing.

"No need to worry about him," the king said. "He is a living organism. A woodfish, you see? Named after those still fossils from the dry world where you come from. Behaves in much the same manner. Hence the name. Genius, genius… I tell you. Cha-kha!"

"You mean this…woodfish needs my carbon dioxide as much as I need its oxygen?"

"Precisely, my lad!" the king said. "It's no wonder you were chosen. Splendid, splendid. Very, very smart, indeed."

With a darting gaze and increased awareness of his environment, Clifton asked, "Chosen for what, Highness?"

A brief flash of regret scrolled across the king's face, replaced by a nervous laugh. A broad smile revealed white teeth too big for his mouth, like sheep crammed into a squished pen.

"Chosen? Why, chosen… for a banquet, of course. And—" he added, pointing a finger in Clifton's face, "special."

He laughed again.

Clifton had no idea why.

Merservants set shell plates, coral utensils, and goblets onto the seaweed tablecloth. Large fossil arrangements made for colorful centerpieces, that fish swam around in search of food.

"Your Highness, why am I here?"

King Gwyddno settled on the seafloor, pulling Clifton down with him. "Here, set this around your waist," he said, handing Clifton a coral belt. "That way, you won't float away."

Clifton strapped the heavy belt in place, that kept him pinned comfortably to the ocean floor. He stared at the king, who seemed to be smiling for no apparent reason. "Your Highness?"

King Gwyddno turned, his eyes wide. "Oh. Didn't see you there. You are a sneaky lad, aren't you?"

Clifton shook his head. "I'm not sure what you mean. I've been standing here the whole time."

The king leaned in close, his face inches from Clifton's, his eyes sharp and alert. "Word travels fast through the land and seas." He nodded as if his explanation was sufficient and thoughtfully stroked his pencil-thin mustache. "You needed help, so I sent my two best mers to save you from that dreadful serpent, though I'm afraid your friend wasn't so lucky, you see? Cha-kha!"

Clifton narrowed his eyes. "He wasn't my friend."

"Even better. Less mourning." Edging toward the banquet table, the king said, "That is why, you see? I saved your life, so you are indebted to me."

The king scrutinized the table as Clifton took in what he'd said. "No, actually. You're wrong, Highness."

"Excuse me, young man? I am never wrong unless you ask my late wife. She disagrees."

"Not to sound ungrateful or anything, but I saw your two best mer long before I saw the sea serpent. I heard them singing from onboard the ship."

"Lovely voices, haven't they? Mesmerizing indeed."

"No, I mean... Yes, they 're lovely, but—I saw them before I needed help. What were they doing circling the ship if you sent them to help me?"

The king's face turned beet red, and he marched toward Clifton, who took an instinctive step back, just as a merman passed between them, carrying colorful desserts to a side table. Bright cakes trimmed with fish eggs and seaweed stole the king's attention like a cartoon character. King Gwyddno wriggled his nose, then let out a small burp.

"Excuse me," he said, as if he had't been planning to attack

Clifton. He skittered toward the dessert table. "Splendid mind you have, my lad. Nothing gets past you, does it?" His voice trailed as he inspected the confectioneries.

Clifton stood alone amidst the bustle of the banquet setup. Everything appeared fine. Happy, beautiful faces prepared an extravagant celebration to welcome him to their city. Their loony leader, King Gwyddno, tested the desserts. Mermaids had saved his life, but something didn't feel right. Something was off. An element out of place, like a word he couldn't remember, lying on the tip of his tongue.

"Psst..."

Clifton turned in the direction of the sound without seeing anyone.

"You. Boy." A large bush of seaweed shook. "Come here," it said.

Leery, Clifton buoyed to the talking bush. He peered between the layers of seaweed but still couldn't see anything, except the arm that reached out, grabbed him, and yanked him inside.

Chapter Forty
Pearl of the Sea

T he mergirl couldn't have been much older than Clifton, if
merpeople showed their age the same as humans. She had
hair the color of seafoam, a cute nose, and big green eyes,
which Clifton couldn't look away from.

"You are not safe here."

Clifton sighed, intoxicated by her melodic voice, unable
to understand her warning of danger.

"You must leave the city before it is too late."

He wore a relaxed grin, his eyes bright and glossy. "Can't.
Stuck here. Don't wanna go. Wanna stay with you."

The mergirl huffed. "Really? Unbelievable." She shuffled
through a pouch strapped across her chest to retrieve two blue
stones. "This will smart," she said, shoving them into both Clifton's

ears.

"Ouch! What was that for?"

"To block my enchantment. They're silencing stones, the only relics which will protect a boy from the voice of a Siren."

"You're a...Siren?"

The mergirl nodded.

"But I thought Sirens killed men."

"They do. Lucky for us, I'm still a girl, and you're just a boy." She took Clifton's hand. "You're not safe here. You must leave straight away."

"How am I not safe?"

"King Gwyddno Garanhir knows you have the Arrow of Light. He wants it."

"Is that why he sent the two mers to the surface?"

She nodded.

"Why didn't he take it from me when we were alone?"

"Because the arrow can't be taken from you."

"That's not true. Some sailor stole it right out of my bag on the ship." The mergirl's hair danced all around her, and even with the silencing stones, Clifton found it hard to concentrate.

"Yes, but you were still on board. It hadn't really been stolen, only changed hands."

Clifton wrinkled his nose. "But he saved my life. I don't understand. Couldn't he have let the sea serpent eat me and taken the arrow that way?"

"Do you even know what comes out of your mouth?" She laughed, a dreamy twinkling sound, and his hand moved to his ear until she swatted it away. "Leave it."

Clifton nodded.

"Sea serpent's stomachs are pools of acid that would dissolve even something as brilliant and magical as that arrow."

"Then I'm safe; he can't have the Arrow of Light. Why bring me here if he can't have it?"

"I never said he couldn't have it. I said he couldn't take it."

Clifton swallowed the lump in his throat. "Go on."

"There are two ways for the arrow to change possession. The first is for you to freely give it away. The other…" She paused to push his hand away from her hair. "Clifton, please try to listen."

He pulled his hand back; grateful she couldn't see him blush beneath the woodfish.

"The other way is not so pleasant. In death, the arrow is reborn, released from its possessor to find another."

Clifton stopped breathing for a moment, and the woodfish squirmed uncomfortably. "So, he's going to kill me?"

The mergirl shook her head. "You don't understand, Clifton. The arrow protects you. You share a bond with it."

"Doesn't seem to be doing a great job."

"You're alive, aren't you?"

Clifton shrugged. "Yeah. I guess so."

"If he can't convince you to give him the arrow, he will find a way for you to say yes. He will torture you. I'm sorry."

"You're sorry?" Clifton went cold. Another king trying to kill him for the arrow.

"If you die with the arrow in your possession, then no one gains control. The only way to truly take the arrow would be to force you to give it up."

Clifton stared at her through watering eyes. "Why are you telling me this?"

"Because I'm a prisoner here too. If King Gwyddno Garanhir possesses the Arrow of Light, he will rule both the dry world and the world under the sea. He will have the power to resurrect Cantre'r Gwaelod from its place on the seafloor back to the land of the sun. There will be no one to stop him." She lowered her head. "I must leave Cantre'r Gwaelod."

Clifton looked around. Every merperson in sight moved about preoccupied with his or her own task, smiles on their beautiful faces, songs sifting through the sea. But deep-down Clifton knew if he tried to leave their only task would be to stop him. He faced the Siren. "I never asked your name."

"It's Pearl."

"That's really pretty."

She smiled softly. "My name's Clifton—"

"Yes, I know who you are. Clifton Chase from another world, like me."

He stared at her a second longer than he knew he ought to. She really was the most beautiful creature he'd ever seen. "I want to help you get out of here. I don't how, Pearl. Down here, this arrow doesn't do me much good except get me captured by a demented King."

She leaned in close to him. "You're a good catch."

He cleared his throat loudly, wondering if she was being literal or flirting. "If I knew I'd be falling into a deadly trap at the bottom of a mythological world, I'd have grabbed my sword. Then I could get us both out."

"And how could you be so confident your sword would do this?"

"Cause it's not any sword, Pearl. This sword belonged to King Arthur, not that I'd expect you to know who he is."

"You know of Excalibur?" she said, her eyes somehow even wider.

"Well, yeah. Every kid my age has heard the legend of the sword in the stone. How do you know about it?"

"I can see why the arrow chose you now." She squeezed his hand. "If you can trust me, Clifton, we can both escape from this place, but I need you to make me a promise if I save your life."

"Sure. What anything?"

"Promise to give me Excalibur freely."

Clifton's eyes bugged. "Are you crazy? Jeez. Now you sound just like them; you know that?"

Pearl shook her head. "It's not like that at all."

"Why do you want King Arthur's sword?"

"Its magic is the only way I can break the enchantment and escape this place. I have been waiting for the day when it finds its way to me. It seems your choice will determine both of our futures." Her sad face pleaded for help.

"Listen, Pearl. I really wish I could help you, but I don't have Excalibur with me. It's back on the ship."

"The sword answers to you, Clifton. It's enchanted, remember?

I will only help you if you swear to give it to me." She moved closer still, and his heart raced from her proximity. "Please," she said, locking eyes with his. "I will risk my life to help you escape. All I ask for in return is Excalibur."

Clifton took several moments to decide. It wasn't that he didn't want Pearl to have it; it was more about him believing it could be done. How would he get it to her? Would she break her promise if he failed? Finally, realizing he had nothing to lose, he said, "Okay, Pearl. It's a deal. You get me back to my friends, and I'll do whatever I need to do to get you that sword."

"Huzzah!" Pearl said, wrapping her arms around his neck. "Oh, thank you, Clifton."

He held her back, wishing he could take off the woodfish to kiss her. She pulled back. "It's settled then," she said. "You call down Excalibur, and I get you safely out of this realm."

"So...how do I...call upon it?"

"You already have, Clifton. It is coming." Pearl reached out her hand. "Quickly."

Clifton slipped his hand into Pearl's. It was tender, delicate, and he never wanted to let go. They pressed silently between the ruins in the field to the edge of the city square, the banquet tables now set as merpeople arrived and took their seats. King Gwyddno Garanhir swiped the edges of cakes with his pudgy fingers, delightedly licking off algae frosting.

"We swim toward the surface," Pearl said. "Once we reach the city's border, an alarm will sound, and we will have only a few moments to escape. I must know that you will do everything I ask without question."

Clifton nodded.

"Promise me," Pearl said.

"I promise."

Pearl stared at his face, and Clifton's body tingled.

"Before we leave, I want to say thank you," Pearl said.

Clifton's brow furrowed. "For what?"

"I can never repay you for what you have done. Hold your breath."

"Why?"

She leaned in and lifted the woodfish off his mouth and kissed him. He couldn't believe it. He thought he was dreaming again, but this was one dream he didn't want to wake up from. Ever. Pearl pulled away, replaced his squirming mask, and smiled.

"Thank you," she said. Clifton's smile widened as his head tilted back, his eyes closed. "Now, c'mon."

Pearl led away from the city streets and across the sandy embankment of the channel's floor. It was a clear shot to the forest-lined perimeter of Cantre'r Gwaelod since the merpeople gathered at the banquet awaiting their guest of honor. "Are you ready?" she asked.

"I guess so."

"Take off your belt. It will keep you tied to the bottom."

Clifton unhooked the heavy belt, the sense of weightlessness rapidly returning.

With one last look, Pearl said, "No matter what happens, I am glad that we met."

"Me, too. I hope we see each other again."

Pearl smiled. "Here we go." She charged out of the covering up toward the city's invisible borders. "Swim harder!"

Clifton kicked his legs while Pearl dragged him toward the murky darkness of the open sea. In his mind, he could hear the merpeople below chattering and whispering, "He's leaving. She's taking him away." The alarm sounded, a shrill honk blaring through conch shells that penetrated the water in blurry sound waves. "Stop, Clifton Chase!" the merpeople chanted as one, their voices growing louder and louder. "Stop, Clifton Chase!"

Clifton kicked harder. He looked over his shoulder and screamed. Reams of merpeople swam full force after him and Pearl. But instead of the glorious, beautiful creatures that had greeted him, they had distorted into hideous monsters with metallic green skin and clawed hands. Their beady eyes stared ahead without blinking, reminding Clifton of the eyes of dead fish. Rows of sharp, spiky teeth had grown inside their gaping black mouths.

Clifton turned toward the endless expanse of sea, mirroring a starless night on land. In the darkness, he swore he saw a star, a pinprick of light shining through the water, twinkling and winking. It moved closer, grew larger, and Clifton realized it was the blade of Excalibur.

"There it is!" he shouted

"We'll never make it like this," Pearl said. "I'm letting go of you."

"No, you can't."

"Good-bye, Clifton Chase. See you soon."

She propelled him upward and he kicked as hard as he could, watching as she disappeared into the darkness. He imagined Pearl landing in the clutches of the metallic monsters, a traitor, torn to pieces for her actions. Clifton couldn't allow himself to believe that and pushed his thoughts aside, focusing instead on expediting Excalibur's approach, kicking harder through the water.

Excalibur neared. "Go to her," he said, and the sword soared past him and out of sight. Swimming away, for what felt like hours, even days, Clifton envisioned the sword landing in Pearl's tender palm while she bravely battled impossible odds, fighting her way to freedom. But a small piece of Clifton worried the sword simply landed in the sand at the sea's bottom, where it lay buried beside the beautiful Siren who had saved his life.

With a flash of light, Clifton's thoughts were shaken, and his eyes closed against the brilliance. Spinning through what felt like thick ice, Clifton wondered if he died as everything disappeared, and he was left in a deep void.

Chapter Forty-One
Constance & Prudence

"**I**s 'e breathin'?" a cheeky voice asked.

"I dunno," a slow voice responded.

"Whadawedo?" said the cheeky one.

"I dunno," the slower one repeated.

"Is there anything ya do know?" insulted cheeky. There was a pause. "Yeah,—prob'ly."

With his eyes closed, Clifton listened to two voices he assumed were female. He had somehow made it out of the English Channel alive, out of the clutches of the sharp-toothed merpeople.

Pearl.

He wondered if she'd survived the attack, if Excalibur reached her in enough time for her to save herself. He hoped. He wouldn't be alive if it weren't for her sacrifice.

"Well, as much 'elp as you've been, I'd be better ta stir the pot than to stare at 'im," the cheeky voice said, falling off.

"And I'd be better to stare at 'im than to eat what yur stirrin' in the pot!" the slower one said, a smile to her voice.

"Baah!" Bare feet shuffled across the floor.

Clifton opened his eyes to face a worn wall, his back to the two women. With the air saturated with cooking onions, he wondered if he, too, would be better off not eating what was in the pot. A towering shadow crossed the wall, and Clifton had the terrifying thought that maybe *he* would be going into the pot with those onions.

He gulped gravel.

The arguing pair seemed to have left the room. Clifton turned his head. The wall in front of him ended where a large plank jutted out from it. Straw bunched from the edges. The ceiling loomed high above him. He was in a barn, or at least that's what it resembled. Clifton rolled over to his other side, feeling the hay bale crunch beneath him. The hay's sweet smell layered beneath the onions made him think of the monsters layered beneath the sweet mermaids. How had he escaped? How had he gotten here? His clothes hung beside him, but he didn't see the Arrow of Light anywhere. He hoped he hadn't lost it again.

"Look, 'e's awake," came a slow voice.

"I can see that. Ya don't think I can see that?" cheeky responded.

"'ow do I know what ya can see?"

The voices drifted closer, close enough to where Clifton should have seen someone, but he didn't see anyone. "Hello?" he called.

"'e can't see us," the slow woman said.

"'ow do ya know that?" asked cheeky.

"I dunno."

"Oh, really?"

"Who's there?" Clifton sat up on the hay bale.

"I'll be a canary's mum. 'e *can't* see us," said cheeky. "What are we gonna do?"

"I dunno."

"Ya really are useless, ain't ya?"

Clifton reached for his clothes, thankful they were dry, and got dressed beneath the cover, which was so rough it probably had been an old feed bag. He jumped, startled by unseen hands clapping off to his right side.

"Got it. Jus' figured it out. We gone invisible again," said the slow woman.

"Oh, dear."

In the snap of a finger, two identical women materialized, with dark hair pulled into coiled buns, both robust, both smiling.

And, both giants.

"I'm Prudence," said the cheeky one. "This is Constance."

"And yur Clifton Chase," Constance said.

"We've 'eard so much aboutcha," added Prudence.

"And the Arrow of Light wicha carry."

"You've seen it?" Clifton asked. "Where is it now?"

"Oh, we 'ave it in a safe place, don't we Constance?"

"I dunno."

"'Ow can ya not know? Yur the one put the spell on it to be invisible. And a jolly good job ya done, spillin' it all over us as well," Prudence scoffed.

"Why don't ya jus' go stir yur pot," Constance said, waving Prudence away. She turned to Clifton. "Ya 'ungry, luv?"

Clifton looked toward the hearth, at the steaming pot the size of a washing machine and shook his head. "No, thanks."

"Prob'ly better thatcha don't," Constance said.

"Suit yerselves," Prudence said. "That's more for me."

Clifton got out from under the sheet and stood, his head reaching just below Constance's waist. He craned his neck. "How did I get here?"

"The arrow broughtcha 'ere," Prudence said. She looked over her shoulder with a grin and stirred the onions. "It will always save ya."

"Why did it bring me here?"

"'Cause that's what Simurgh told it tado," Constance said.

"Simurgh?"

"'A course. Whodya think persuades the Arrow of Light?" Prudence asked. "Ya control it and it does whatcha says, but as long as them feathers are upon it, it retains a bond to Simurgh. That's where the real power lies."

Clifton rubbed his chin for a moment. "So that's why King Richard and King Gwyddno want it so badly? To control Simurgh?"

"That's why everyone who desires power wants the arrow, and is chasin' ya, for that matter," Constance said. "Simurgh knows no boundaries. She sees all and can be anywhere. The possessor of the arrow can defeat any enemy. Even death, if they can understand how."

"Then why did the arrow choose me?"

"You'll 'ave to ask Simurgh that question yerself," Prudence said. "And lucky for ya she's on 'er way."

Chapter Forty-Two

Bow and Arrow

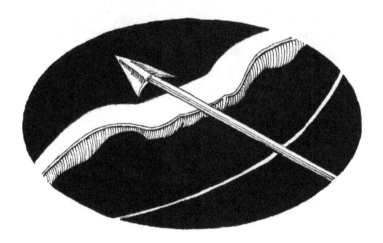

C lifton stood on the back porch of the barnhouse, drinking a cup of hot tea. Thoughts spun around in his head, weaving as thread while he waited for Simurgh's.

Why *had* the arrow chosen him?

Prudence and Constance fought inside the house; their voices carried through the open door with great gusto. Clifton imagined even those in the valley far, far beneath them would know that Constance always served tea with warm milk, while Prudence insisted milk was too heavy and tea must instead have lemon.

Still, the thought of seeing Simurgh perked him up, the face of a friend among these strangers. It felt like a lifetime ago when he was back in his own bedroom, in his own time, with his mom in the kitchen and Pierce coloring in the living room.

In the distance, a shape covered the sun. He focused on it until Simurgh came into view, just as the giants said she would. She landed in the green grass on the hill beyond the porch. Clifton crossed to the side gate stairwell, bounding down to the grass in as few steps as possible.

"Clifton, my dear friend," she said.

"Simurgh!" He threw his arms around her enormous avian body. "It's so great to see you." He stepped back. "Where have you been?"

"I have been where I was needed to be, although now I am needed here. Have the twins treated you well?"

"Oh, yeah. They've been great. But I can't say that's true for the way they treat each other. I mean, I thought my cousins were bad. They're always fighting. But that's nothing compared to these two."

Simurgh laughed. "Not much changes in the world." She looked up to the porch and Clifton followed her gaze.

"What an honor to be in the presence of the twins of Mount Carnel," Simurgh said.

"'ello, Simurgh," Constance said. Turning to Prudence she added, "I told ya it was 'er."

"An 'onor to 'ave ya 'ere," Prudence said, then responded to Constance, "I never said it wasn't."

"Didentcha?"

"Well, I dunno."

"Oh! Why I stay 'ere wicha is beyond me."

"A mutual feelin', I can assure ya."

"Ahem. Excuse me, fair maidens of Mount Carnel," Simurgh said, bowing deeply. "Though your hospitality is unmatched by any in the land, the time for departure is upon us and we must make haste."

"'A course," Prudence said.

"Anything for ya, Simurgh," Constance added.

"I am most grateful. If you please, I must get the boy moving, so I request his belongings be returned, along with any others you may care to add."

With simultaneous nods, Prudence and Constance retreated into the barnhouse, leaving Clifton and Simurgh alone again.

"Where are we going now?" Clifton asked.

"To meet up with our comrades. They are on the brink of a war; one they will lose if we do not reach them soon."

Clifton scratched his cheek. "Simurgh, there's something I've been meaning to ask you."

She turned to face him, her eyes sparkling. "I know the answers you seek. But they are not mine to give. Only you can answer those questions."

The giants reappeared in the doorway of the barn, descended the steps, and crossed through the grass. Prudence carried the Arrow of Light, or was it Constance, he couldn't tell. But it didn't matter. One of them had it.

"'ere are the things we found ya with," Prudence said. She handed Clifton the arrow and the silencing stones.

Clifton ran his fingers across the smooth blue stones. "Had almost forgotten about these," he said, and for an instant, his heart grew heavy thinking of Pearl.

"And 'ere is something we wantcha to 'ave," Constance said, handing Clifton a wooden bow etched with strange symbols. "The bow of Jehu, used to shoot an arrow through the 'eart of a terrible king, and restore peace and 'onor to the people of 'is land."

"It will serve ya well," Prudence said. "Shoots straight, ev'ry time."

Both women smiled down at him. "Thank you," Clifton whispered. He ran his fingers over the string. It felt like a white-hot ember though it cooled instantly to the touch.

"Your gift is most appropriate," Simurgh said. "I am sure it will be of great use when the time is most desperate."

"Thank you," Clifton said.

"Good-bye, Clifton," Constance said, bending down and kissing his cheek.

"Best of luck, to ya," Prudence said, kissing his other cheek.

"'e's gonna need it," Constance said, under her breath.

For once Prudence didn't disagree with her sister, and Clifton slumped as the bow became heavy in his hands.

"Clifton," Simurgh said, "our time is up. Climb aboard."

He looked one last time at the two giants while climbing onto Simurgh's broad back, running his fingers through her familiar soft down. He waved good-bye as Simurgh leapt into the air. The giants waved back. It was the first time Prudence and Constance had not been fighting since Clifton opened his eyes that morning. And he couldn't help but think how sweet they looked waving at him, standing in the valley, arm in arm.

Chapter Forty-Three
Reunited

C lifton forgot how high Simurgh flew and how cold the dense clouds became. He clutched her soft feathers in his fists and even though the hot sun beat on his back, his teeth chattered.

"How far are we going?" he asked, over the rushing wind.

"Not much farther. Henry has made camp at the Cistercian Abbey of Merevale in Atherstone."

"An abbey? So, they reached port?"

"Nearly three weeks ago."

"How can that be? I just fell overboard yesterday."

"Not true, child. The journey to Cantre'r Gwaelod is long, and Time is not welcome within its borders. You have been gone for nineteen days."

Clifton's head swam, digesting what Simurgh said. Nineteen days? That meant he'd been gone from home for almost a month. His poor mom. She'd probably forced some worker at the T.G. Lee Company to plaster his face on the side of every milk carton in the US. He shook his head, a sour taste in his mouth. He was never going to leave this place. He had no idea how to get home. But Simurgh knew. She knew more than she cared to share, like a safe with secrets locked away.

"You knew I was in Cantre'r Gwaelod because of your connection to the arrow, didn't you?" Clifton asked, his words sharp.

"Yes. I did."

"Why didn't you come rescue me? I was in serious trouble."

"Things do not always come to us in the way we expect, but that does not mean what we expect does not come."

Clifton closed his eyes, a headache pounding his temples as if they were timpani drums. Descending, Simurgh passed through misty clouds coating Clifton's already goosebumped skin. When they came through, the greens and browns of earth lay beneath them, canyons, valleys, rivers, and mountains.

"So, you're saying that you *did* rescue me?" Clifton asked.

"Not I, for I do not swim."

Clifton's jaw clenched, the timpani resounding into a tribal war dance. "A Siren saved me. Her name was Pearl."

"Your world is limited by your perspective, young Clifton. Help comes in many forms and at many costs, even the ultimate price of death. But if you believe it, it always comes."

Clifton realized the answer to the riddle. "You told her to save me."

"Close, but not quite."

Clifton rubbed his head, stretching his neck to loosen the muscles. Pearl wasn't told, but she did save him. Because of Excalibur. "You planted the thought in my head. About Arthur's sword."

"Now you're seeing clearly."

"But...how?"

"We cannot always know the wisdom working on our behalf, nor do we always know the answers to our most pressing questions. Sometimes we must find satisfaction in simply knowing that someone greater is looking out for us and learn instead to show gratitude."

Clifton's cheeks flushed with heat. "I'm sorry to have seemed ungrateful, Simurgh. I appreciate everything you've done. Thank you."

Simurgh laughed sending tremors through her belly, that vibrated up her back and shook Clifton. Her laughter somehow reminded him of Pearl. He wondered if she had lived. He really didn't want to know, just in case she hadn't made it. He didn't think he could handle that.

They flew closer to the woodlands. The trees began to take shape, and the valleys showed their depth. A square manor spread out in the open space with a brick gatehouse extending around the perimeter of the property. Spires jutted up like miniature mountain peaks. Exterior halls with many windows connected each building of the abbey, reminding him of train-cars parked in a depot.

The bricks came into focus. The tiles on the roof. Simurgh made her descent into the atrium within the boundary wall, and the abbey doors swung open. Clifton's friends rushed out to greet him, first Richard, then Edward, followed by Henry and Elizabeth holding hands, with Jasper close behind. Finally, Dane exited, smoking his pipe. Wearing his crooked little smile, he waved at Clifton, who smiled back. He was so happy to see everyone. They had grown into a sort of family.

As Simurgh touched the ground, she whispered, "She did not die, you know."

Clifton's heart fluttered. He jumped off Simurgh's back to look into her all-knowing eyes, like two violet crystal balls. "Pearl?" he asked, his throat tight. "She lived?"

"The sword reached her in time."

Clifton laughed as his friends came over to welcome him back. He couldn't have been happier. Not only reunited with old friends but satisfied in knowing that his new friend, Pearl, had survived.

Chapter Forty-Four

The Night Before

N ight fell, and most of the residents of the abbey had already gone to bed. Clifton lay on a blanket, staring at hundreds of twinkling stars in the cloudless sky. Jasper lit a fire in the field outside the hall-lined atrium within Merevale's walled border. The dry wood snapped and popped as the fire caught. Henry's army of nearly five-thousand men encamped across the abbey grounds with hundreds of fires burning like falling stars.

Clifton paid attention to Edward, who used a sturdy stick to draw in the dirt. "According to the Stanley brothers," Edward said, "Uncle's forces are not far off, perhaps here in Leicester." He pointed to a spot in the dirt near a clump of grass. "This puts the abbey here." The stick landed near a rock. Connecting the two landmarks by running the branch through the dirt, he added, "If we leave at dawn, heading southeast on horseback, we should meet somewhere near Ambion Hill." He drew a large circle near the center point.

"That is assuming King Richard also breaks camp before dawn and has knowledge of our whereabouts," Henry said.

"I have no doubt that he does."

While Edward and Henry continued planning, Elizabeth came and sat beside Clifton. "So, you were really in Cantre'r Gwaelod?" Her eyes grew large in her delicate face.

Clifton straightened up. "Yup, apparently for longer than I thought."

"What was it like? I have heard the city is made of oyster shells, and the streets are paved in gold. What of the mermaids? Are they as beautiful as legend says?"

"Sort of. I mean, when I was swimming for my life to escape, they became these horrible monsters." He paused, then shook his head. "I can't even think about it for too long."

"Oh, my," Elizabeth said, her face turned in disappointment. "Were they all that way?"

Clifton shook his head. "No. There was this one mergirl…." He stared off into his memories and found Pearl. He looked back to Elizabeth with a genuine smile. "Now, she was beautiful."

"Who was beautiful?" Richard asked, plopping down beside his sister.

Elizabeth held his hand. "The mergirl Clifton met in Cantre'r Gwaelod. He is telling about his adventure."

"How beautiful exactly?" Richard asked.

Clifton envisioned Pearl's face, her soft green eyes, her porcelain skin, her soothing voice. "More beautiful than words can say."

"Enough about mergirls," Elizabeth interrupted as her eyes trained on Clifton. "Having seawater constantly in your skin is bound to make anyone prune up in no time at all." She swatted at the air; her cheeks rosy. "Tell me about the city. Is it how legend describes?"

"It was this ancient, underwater city. It doesn't get much cooler than that."

"Interesting. I have heard speculation that the temperature drops below freezing in the depths," Richard said.

Clifton chuckled. "Nah, man. Not that kind of cool. Waaay cool."

"Waaay cool," Richard mimicked with a chuckle.

Clifton looked at Elizabeth. "And about the legend, the roads were made of crushed shells, not gold. At least, not in the part of the city where I was."

"And what of the palace?"

"Oh, that was awesome. Like being in Ancient Rome or something. It was covered in ginormous corals and crunched up shells that could have been oyster shells, I guess."

"Your language is so strange, Clifton," Elizabeth said. "It takes some getting used to."

"Ditto," Clifton said.

"Ditto," Elizabeth echoed.

Dane smoked his pipe, his usual evening entertainment. "It's impossible to escape from Cantre'r Gwaelod," he said. Everybody stopped laughing. "No one ever has."

"Then how do people know to describe it, dwarf?" Elizabeth asked, her lips pressed in a white slash.

"According to Clifton, they don't."

"Well, what about you?" Clifton asked. "How did you escape from all those guards in Droffilc Tower? Seemed a pretty impossible escape to me."

Dane eyed Clifton. His nose twitched. "Let's just say, I got lucky, 'tis all."

"No such thing as luck, only fate," Edward said.

Clifton looked up at Edward, who had overheard his conversation with Dane, then turned his attention to Dane's soured face. "Besides Dane, you said you'd tell me all about it when the time was right."

Dane pulled his hat down over his eyes and leaned back on the cold earth. "Well, the time ain't right."

"But you did escape," Clifton said.

"'Aye. And now I wish to escape to the blackness of the insides of me eyelids."

Elizabeth huffed. "Dwarves."

Clifton smiled. "You can be a real pain in the neck, Dane."

"'Aye."

"Guess that makes you like family." Clifton and Elizabeth laughed.

"Do you miss your mum and dad?" Richard asked.

Clifton grew very still, and a heaviness replaced his laughter. "I sure do. A whole bunch. And my little brother. It feels like forever since I've seen my family."

"At least you will see them again someday." A tear rolled down Richard's cheek. Elizabeth wrapped her arm around him, pulling him into her chest, where he quietly sobbed.

"There, there, little brother. Tomorrow is a new day. And each new day brings us that much closer to seeing Dad and Mum again."

"Especially tomorrow," Dane said.

Clifton laughed nervously. "Thought you said you were going to sleep."

"Who can sleep with all this jibber-jabbin?"

"Jeez, Dane. What's your problem?"

Dane pushed back his hat and sat up. He looked Clifton in the eye. "Tomorrow we face King Richard on the battlefield. Many lives will be lost, and much blood will be spilled."

Clifton again saw the oil painting in his mind's eye; the ground still stained crimson with blood.

"You may have the Arrow of Light in your possession, lad, but ya lack the heart to understand it's meaning." He leaned closer. "Do not think for one moment that the arrow will save ya if you don't know how to use it."

Dane stood and stormed away, leaving Clifton sitting by a fire that suddenly felt cold. Richard sniffled loudly, stifling his tears, and Elizabeth took him into the abbey. Clifton forced back his own tears.

Could he really die tomorrow?

Henry and Edward now sat around a different fire, moving between the groups of men, mapping out strategies as they planned for tomorrow's battle.

Tomorrow's war.

Clifton had never felt so alone in all his life. What purpose would there be for the arrow to have chosen him if he could die? He looked over the plans Edward had scratched into the dirt. They were real.

And he faced a real battle against a real king in the morning, not some battle in an old movie or a history lesson. He shivered, wondering what the outcome would be. He knew now that he *was* part of something greater than himself. And that he was the one expected to kill King Richard.

Chapter Forty-Five

Preparations

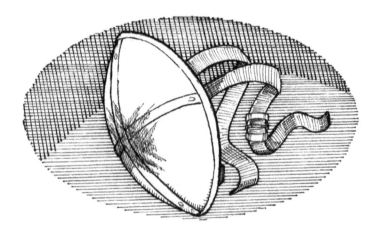

C lifton opened his eyes. Dawn peeked above the horizon, and the camp already stirred with movement. Birds chirped happily like it was any other morning although Clifton didn't feel so happy. The night's dying fires smoldered hot embers into the earth, and pain grew in the pit of his stomach as the men dressed for battle.

Edward approached Clifton, carrying a clay cup. "Good-morrow, Clifton." He handed him hot Dropwater. "I hope you slept well."

Clifton hadn't slept well at all, his night one long continuous nightmare starring King Richard, his face contorted and writhing into a demon's. "Not so much," he said, taking the drink. "Thanks." He sipped it with a grimace. The Dropwater tasted bitter and needed sugar, nothing like Liv's back at the dwarves' cottage.

"Our morning meal has been prepared and served. The monks are most generous."

Clifton spied the makeshift wooden table where monks ladled white blobs of oats into bowls.

"I'm really not very hungry," Clifton said.

"Hungry or not, you need to eat. The battlefield is a draining place, and we do not know when our next meal may come. It is best to enter with a full belly so as not to make war with one's belly as opposed to the enemy."

His stomach already felt like a miniature battlefield. He held the Dropwater mug for warmth but didn't drink it.

Dane crossed the field in Clifton's direction. "Here, lad. Yer battle garments."

He carried a smock, a coat of mail, and a helmet. Clifton couldn't wrap his brain around it. These were clothes he saw in books or on dummies at museums. But here, all the men wore them. And for many they would become their burial shrouds. Clifton felt sick.

"Why do I need all this?" Clifton asked.

"To live," Dane said with a smirk, thrusting the pile into Clifton's hands before marching off.

Clifton remembered pictures of medieval men riding into battle, their long-sleeved tunics layered with mesh chainmail, or fifteenth-century arrow-proof vests as he liked to think of them, hanging down over leggings and boots like the ones he wore.

Studying the men around him, Clifton finally figured out how to layer the garments. He stood in his new costume. The material pulled heavy and awkward, like a quarterback playing in pads for the first time. The helmet fit snugly though it would take some getting used to since his peripheral vision was sliced at the edges. He turned his arms to catch each angle, stared at his chest, his legs. A thought struck him, and his breath caught in his chest. He was now the boy in the painting, missing only a red marking on his chainmail.

A large man with a mustache that connected to a long beard hobbled over, a bucket in one hand, a bunch of straw attached to a stick by a thin leather strap in the other. "May God be with you," he said, dipping the makeshift brush into the bucket. He painted a mark across Clifton's chest. Red paint dripped to the ground beneath him.

Now his chainmail was marked. There would be no escaping the oil painting coming to life. Panicked breaths filled his lungs. Clifton grew dizzy.

"What's the matter with you?" a man asked, placing his enormous palm on Clifton's back, sending him stumbling forward and colliding with Elizabeth. The clay mugs of steaming Dropwater she carried went flying through the air. Black sludge coated Clifton's pant leg and Elizabeth's pale green smock. She screamed as Clifton tackled her to the ground, where they both tumbled in the mud.

"Get off the princess, you fool!"

"I can't. I'm stuck." He couldn't budge.

They were attached somewhere, maybe his belt with her lace piping, and he couldn't even try to work it free since his helmet had shifted, the eye holes now exposing the bridge of his nose and temple. "I'm so sorry, Elizabeth."

She kept squirming.

"Elizabeth!" Henry said from a short distance off.

Footsteps approached. Someone tugged hard on Clifton's chainmail. What was left of his world yanked out from beneath him. Now on his feet, he threw off his helmet. The guy who had started this whole mess held him tight by pinching his chainmail and twisting it up the way someone would a dog collar on a chain.

"Let go of me," Clifton shouted.

"Not on your life," the man said.

Henry helped Elizabeth to her feet, her dress splotched with mud and clumped with pine needles.

"Are you all right, my dear?" Henry asked, helping her brush the pine needles away.

She shook her leaf-matted head; her cheek indented with red lines from Clifton's helmet. Many of the nearby soldiers had stopped their preparations and gathered around.

"Elizabeth. My Lady." Everyone turned to look at Clifton, whose skin turned very hot. "Please, forgive me. I—I... I am so very sorry."

Somehow, she smiled. "Just a bit of mud," she managed. "Will you excuse me?" She retreated to the monastery.

Henry glared at him, then marched away. The men quickly lost interest and went back to their breakfasts. Clifton couldn't remember ever being so embarrassed in his entire life.

The man who started it all released his grip. "Best get your footing secure before you do that on the battlefield and get someone killed." He grunted and left.

"Thanks for that word of advice," Clifton yelled after him. "Very encouraging."

Edward and Richard bounced over. "Clifton, what in the world happened?" Edward asked.

"I don't even know, man."

"Having a bit of practice, were you?" Richard asked with a grin. "Thought my sister the best candidate for a tackle?" He couldn't hold his laughter any longer.

"Enough, brother," Edward said, wiping a leaf off Clifton's shoulder. "Even the great lion can trip on its own legs. Come. It is time to march."

Clifton bent over and lifted his helmet from the ground, dusting off the dirt. "What am I doing here? I'm not ready for this," he said to himself. As he slid on his helmet and gathered his gear, he began to pray.

Chapter Forty-Six
The March

Dane helped Clifton onto his horse, a black mare with a white patch of fur running down her face. Clifton's chainmail clanked, like nickels in a dryer, and his helmet rubbed incessantly against the bridge of his nose and cheeks. The mare snorted as Dane steadied her.

"Best hold on," Dane said. Clifton grabbed onto the only thing he could, the mid-section of the little man. "Not so hard, lad. You'll suffocate me before we reach the battle."

The army stood assembled across the grounds, an impressive bunch of men holding shields etched with the Tudor Crest, a red dragon against a black background. Clifton's cold skin broke into a sweat as the procession moved away from the safety of Merevale into the uncertainty of war, the Arrow of Light tucked securely inside the quiver, his bow strapped tightly across his chest.

As they passed the abbey, Elizabeth stood in the entranceway beside the guardhouse. She wore a crème colored gown, her long, blonde hair shining in the early morning sun. She waved a white lace handkerchief to the passing soldiers as a tear rolled down her cheeks.

The men passed through the gate into the open countryside. The serenity of the green fields and dew-covered grass seemed unnaturally calm as if attempting to persuade the Loyalists to avoid the blood-soaked grounds they would soon be lying across, like Sirens calling out to sailors from the rocks.

Pearl.

Images of the beautiful mergirl flooded Clifton's mind if only to give him something to hope for. After all, she survived impossible odds and escaped the hands of the enemy.

Daylight spread through the trees and across the unmarked path. Henry and Edward led their men bravely. It was quiet except for the clomping hooves crunching pebbles and leaves as they marched.

Was Richard waiting for them, alerted by one of his many spies? If so, Clifton hoped Henry and Edward were prepared for the assault. He looked ahead to see the princes, with their heads held high, riding their steed. He wished he had their same confidence and courage as they moved toward the battlefield. They would all be facing King Richard today; only the princes would be facing an uncle who betrayed them, too. Even with all the pain, he had caused and all he had taken from them; he was still their blood relative. The reality hit him again. They were facing the king today. How would they ever beat him?

"I called to the guards from the hall," Dane said, from out of nowhere. "They were well on their way to drunk by the time we arrived to Drofflic Tower. Ya went running up the stairwell, like a wildebeest, and none of them even noticed ya, so I knew if ya didn't mess things up, you'd prolly be okay."

The mare stumbled on a rock. "C'mon, now. No horse a mine be trippin' on their own legs." He steered the mare to a clearer pass. "So, up they jump, swords unsheathed and drawn, chairs slamming to the ground in a chorus. And I thought to meself, they're gonna kill me."

Clifton hung on his words, remembering the same feeling when the guard caught him by the leg in the window.

"They came at me," Dane continued. "And I swung back at 'em, twisting through the spaces between their legs and stabbing at whatever I could reach." He paused. "Then, something hit me."

"What, like a sword?"

"Not literally, boy. Honestly, I don't know what happened." Dane pushed the mare harder as the company of horses picked up their pace, the clomping now sounding like the click-clack of a train on the tracks.

"It was as if the lights turned out for them, but it was clear as day to me. The way they staggered around, with their hands reaching out in front of them. Never seen anything like it. So, I took advantage of my luck and did what needed to be done." He shivered, and his voice trailed off. "Strangest thing..."

They passed several of the springs feeding the Sence Brook, and the hard soil changed to marshlands. A ridge of high ground spread out in both directions ahead, past a deserted hamlet, then sloped down to level off to meet the banks of the river. It was Ambion Hill. Clifton recognized it from the pictures on the internet.

It was where King Richard III was going to die.

Chapter Forty-Seven

The Players

T he crest of the hill was lined with royal soldiers, greater in number than Henry's army, even with the additional reserves the Stanley brothers brought. King Richard's men carried scores of weapons, swords and shields, bows and arrows, and large catapults stockpiled with ammunition.

"Take yer arrow," Dane said. "Be prepared to ready yer bow. But dontcha be shooting in haste."

Clifton reached back into his quiver, lost his balance, and started to fall off the horse. Dane reached out, caught him by his chainmail, and pulled him upright.

"Keep yerself together, lad."

"I'm trying, Dane," Clifton said defensively.

Clifton looked around at the faces of the Loyalist army, stern, proud men showing no signs of the intimidation and fear that plagued Clifton. Someone hollered, and the main army marched ahead across the boggy field in a single, larger division.

"Who's he?" Clifton asked, pointing to the older man doing the hollering.

"He is the Earl of Oxford," Richard said, his horse a few strides away. "He is an experienced and gifted leader. Even King Richard's men know of his reputation and war record, which is precisely why Henry chose him to lead."

"What about them?" Clifton asked, pointing in the distance at men grouped by their weapons.

"The archers are Welsh mainly, and the men holding spears and clubs are Scottish mercenaries. The smaller divisions on the wings are English men-at-arms. But we are all the same, each loyal to my father."

The soldiers crossed the Sence Brook, driving toward Ambion Hill. Dane led the mare off the path, followed by Richard.

"What are we doing?" Clifton asked, watching the others pass.

"Waiting," Dane said.

Richard shouted words of encouragement and expressions of gratitude to the men waving at the soldiers as they passed. Some looked Clifton's age. Others older than dirt. But the men were strong and determined, and Clifton held his head a little higher. Several of the men broke from the pack at random, moving to join the small band of men forming with Dane, Clifton, and Richard.

"What are we waiting for?" Clifton asked.

"Just be still, lad."

Henry cantered up with Edward beside him. They joined the group as the other men continued to press on toward the hill.

Facing the small band of soldiers perched at the edge of the marsh, Henry said, "Men, it is with great honor that I stand before you. Today, there will be a victor. We will leave this hill having defeated our enemy, or we will die trying."

No one spoke a word. All eyes trained on Henry.

"King Richard's tyranny will soon come to an end."

The small band of soldiers cheered. The Tudor flag waved in the slight breeze, the red dragon dancing and swaying. Clifton thought of the dragon in Èze, with its wicked claws and scorching flames. The image of the dragon on the flag looked comical, a cartoon version doing a poor imitation of the real thing.

"This is the last battle of the War of the Roses. Two kings and their armies will fight to the death on this field." Henry Tudor's eyes narrowed. "On my honor, I swear the blood of King Richard will spill this day, and the ground of Ambion Hill will be forever stained crimson."

More hollers rose from the men, louder and stronger. The horses whinnied and snorted restlessly.

Edward raised his arm, and the men quieted. "It is also our duty to protect Sir Clifton and the Arrow of Light at all costs."

Clifton clutched the arrow to his chest, his throat so dry it hurt to swallow.

"Men, today, we fight. Today we win. Today, my father's name will be restored to its glory!"

The men shouted, chanting in rhythm, their war cry rising even to the peak of Ambion Hill.

"Take ranks," Henry said, and the band of men shifted, filing in to join those marching past.

Chapter Forty-Eight
The King's Arrival

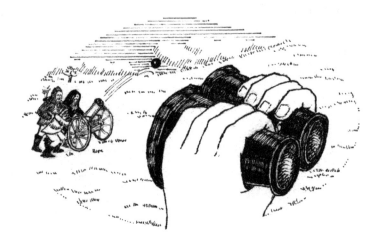

Kqing Richard's men clustered on the crest of Ambion Hill as a group of archers marched across to take their places at the front, the first offensive line to protect the king.

The small division led by Henry and Edward had stopped. Clifton tugged at the cloth, now too tight around his neck. "Uh, Dane, can those arrows reach us?"

"Not likely." He smiled a crooked little grin. "Their bein' on the high ground does gain them a slight advantage in range, if the air holds steady." He pointed ahead. "But ya see how Oxford marches his men with the sun to their backs? That sun be a blindin' force on Richard's men once the Loyalist's arrows start flying."

"But it looks as though we needn't worry," Richard added. "Those men are not in battle formation. It seems uncle did not consider organizing such a large force into an ordered front in such a small space."

Clifton looked to the crest of Ambion Hill. "It does look pretty cramped up there."

"It certainly does," Richard said.

"And look who has just arrived," Henry said, passing an optical instrument to the prince.

"Pass those on," Edward said, taking them from Richard. He peered through the lens. "Uncle." Passing the gadget back to Richard, he said, "Did you take a good look at his face, Richard?" His voice trembled.

Richard stared hard through the lens, then scoffed. "He looks like a rabbit caught in a trap."

"He certainly does," Edward said. "He is probably working out a plan of escape to save his own 'arse."

The brothers laughed, and Clifton smiled at the thought of King Richard shaking in his boots.

"I bet he is soiling his trousers at the great numbers coming to kill him," Richard added.

"I hope so," Edward said. He looked at Henry. "It's time to put things right. We follow you, My Lord."

Henry plodded on his horse to the front of the group and marched ahead.

Clifton let out a nervous laugh. "Sure hope I can do what I was brought here to do."

Dane turned to meet Clifton's eyes. "Hope's not what we need, boy. You *must* do what ya were brought here to do. Or none of us will ever see home again." He turned, pushing the mare to follow the others.

Clifton's hands sweat.

The small band of men brought up the rear as Henry marched them across the boggy ground, through the marsh, the valley, all the way to the base of Ambion Hill to meet the rest of the Loyalist army.

King Richard's archers readied their bows and released. Black lines arced through the sky as the arrows flew toward the English men-at-arms. The main flank crouched, covering themselves with their shields, like turtles in armored shells.

From nowhere, a backwind blew. The arrows teetered, then fell, most never finding their marks. Clifton looked around. Jasper stood where the marsh met the river, a sword held high above his head, as he conjured the winds as he had on the English Channel.

On the top of Ambion Hill, archers shuffled away, replaced by the gunnery of the royal cannons. The soldiers spared no time, and metal balls, like the ones in Flaxton Village, whirred through the air aimed at the winged flanks positioned on the outskirts of Oxford's main army.

"Move!" Oxford shouted. The flanks moved parallel to the artillery until out of reach of the gunner's blows. Once outside the trajectory, Oxford's formidable bowmen directed their attack on the royal army.

"Archers," Oxford said, his arm lifted in the air. The impressive line of Welshmen drew back their strings. "Aim." The archers angled back as one unit, forming a straight unified front. "Loose!" Arrows flew toward the hill, and the king's archers responded with a counterattack. Arrows shot endlessly from both sides. Men caught in the crossfire of the lethal bodkin-headed shafts hit the ground hard. Hand gunners opened fire on both sides. Shouts rose across the field and down Ambion Hill.

"Here we go, lad," Dane said, charging across the field.

The king's men sped down the slope of the hill, the entire vanguard screaming with swords drawn as Henry and his men followed Oxford to meet the front. It was a blur of men-at-arms, armored bodies, pike men, hand gunners, and archers closing in on each other near the foot of the hill. Swords clashed as the close combat butchery carried out with swords, maces, axes, and staff weapons.

They battled fiercely for the crown, for the throne, and Clifton knew, for the Arrow of Light he held in his hand. He watched the men swinging weapons between them, making contact, then falling and dying on both sides.

The ground beneath him gave way as the mare fell over. Clifton hurried out from under the weight of the great steed and lifted his sword. Surrounding him stood Dane and Richard, Henry and

Edward, clashing swords with the king's men and taking out as many royal soldiers as they could.

A soldier charged at Clifton, a brute man with a battle axe. Clifton ducked, barely missing the axe's blunt edge, and he sliced through the air, nicking the man in his calf. Dane jumped on the axe-man's back, wedging his sword deep into the soldier's side. He hung on until the man fell with a thud.

Clifton slashed at soldiers, screaming as his sword clanked against the enemy's, dodging a blow from a mace and cutting into the soldier's arms on his way up. He looked for the king, finding him on the crest of Ambion Hill, their eyes locked.

"I'm going in for Richard," Clifton yelled.

Edward nodded while fighting off a soldier twice his size with his brother's help.

"Dane, cover me," Clifton yelled, dropping to his knees.

King Richard descended the hill surrounded by his guards. His black hair hung to his shoulders beneath a stolen crown. A robe stretched down his back, laying out flat across his horse. Beneath it, the king's body was covered in thick armor with his family crest etched across his glinting breastplate.

Clifton's hands shook as he took off the Bow of Jehu, the string glowing white-hot, and notched the Arrow of Light.

For this moment.

King Richard and his elite guard charged halfway down the hill. The Arrow of Light glowed, the fletching waved, humming with life in his ear. The enemy gained. Clifton had only moments. He pulled taut on the string; the wooden bow pressed firmly in his grasp.

Just a little closer.

In a flash, a loud boom shook him, and he fell to his side. The cannonball barely missed his head. His weapons were thrown, landing several feet away. Clifton jumped up, crawling toward the arrow as King Richard closed in on him. He wasn't going to make it.

The cannonball's impact knocked the princes to the ground, too. The king smiled at his nephews, an insane, demented, terrible smile. "Hello, nephews," he said, circling them.

Richard lay sprawled out across the dirt, his forehead painted with blood.

"Richard!" Edward shouted, jumping to his brother's side.

Clifton turned his attention to the princes. In that split second where he faltered, one of the king's archers already held a drawn bow set on him. He had reached the Arrow of Light, but not the bow.

"Clifton Chase," King Richard said, dismounting from his horse. "It is my pleasure to finally meet you. And watch you die."

"You must be King Richard," Clifton said, sitting up a little. "You're a lot uglier than I expected."

King Richard laughed. "And you are much less intelligent than the others the Arrow of Light has chosen in the past."

King Richard moved closer. From the corner of his eye, Clifton noticed the archer's arms shaking from holding the draw for so long. Clifton knew the feeling. It was exactly how he had felt in Wickham Park waiting to shoot the Arrow of Light for the first time.

Where was Simurgh? Why had she abandoned him? Surely if she were here, none of this would be happening. "So, now what?" Clifton asked. "You kill me, take the arrow, and lock up your nephews again?"

King Richard's smile chilled Clifton's bones. "Not quite. The Arrow of Light holds power if you willingly give it to me."

Clifton shook his head. "Well, that's never gonna happen. I'd rather you killed me."

"If that is the way you would like for this to proceed, I will just have to persuade you otherwise. Guards!"

Several of the king's elite men moved out from behind him.

"Kill the princes," he said.

The soldiers towered over Henry, who covered Richard's still body beneath him.

"No!" Clifton screamed. "Wait!"

"Clifton, no," Henry said.

"Take the arrow," Clifton said, handing it out to the closest soldier. "Just leave my friends alone."

King Richard motioned for his guards to step away from his nephews while a different guard took the arrow from Clifton's hand. "You have chosen wisely, Clifton Chase," said the king, snatching the arrow from his guard. His eyes lit up as the shaft glowed a strange shade of green Clifton had never seen before.

"It's mine," King Richard rasped. "It's mine!"

Thunder clapped and lightning shot through the air, and while Clifton hoped it was one of Jasper's tricks, he knew it was impossible since Jasper stood beside Henry. Terrified soldiers ran in every direction as dark clouds rolled in, and the winds began to gust.

"Kill them all," King Richard said, turning back toward his horse.

Without anyone noticing, Dane launched a poisoned dart through the reed he had snuck to his mouth. It landed in a weak spot in the king's armor, where it cut through his skin. King Richard dropped the Arrow of Light as he stumbled, his guards catching him. Henry threw off the soldiers beside him with Edward and Jasper doing the same.

The king screamed, "Kill him!" His shaking finger pointed right at Clifton.

The quaking arms of the king's archer released. The arrow headed straight for Clifton. He had failed them completely now. He had given the arrow away and cost all of them their lives. The king had won, and Clifton had only changed history for the worse. Who knew what he had done to the future. The arrow inched closer. He was going to die.

That's when Time played tricks on him.

Edward screamed. Horses galloped. Soldiers clashed swords. Sparks flew. The king stumbled. The archer released. Dane stood before Clifton. The dwarf's eyes squinted closed. His mouth missed its crooked grin. He gasped, he winced, his stout body crashed into Clifton's, and they both fell to the marshy ground.

Chapter Forty-Nine
Choices

Clifton screamed. His voice sounded distant. Henry drew his sword and plunged toward the king's guards, taking them down one by one. Edward joined him, slashing through chain mail in quick spurts to take out as many as he could. Together they eliminated the king's guards.

"Dane!" Clifton yelled, throwing off his helmet.

The shaft of the arrow meant for Clifton stuck out from Dane's chest. He lay on the marsh, his blood pooling around him.

"No, Dane. You're gonna be okay," Clifton said, his tears blurring his vision. He took off his chainmail, then his tunic, and balled it up, pressing it against Dane's wound.

Dane winced. "Leave it, lad."

"I won't, Dane. I can't! I can't sit here and watch you die." He remembered his dream vividly, the ledge moving farther and farther away as Dane's blood spread out beneath him on the ground. He couldn't believe it was coming true. What could he do? "Don't leave me," he whispered.

Dane stared up at him, his blue eyes clear, his crooked little smile pronounced. "Not goin' anywhere yet, lad." He breathed air in through closed teeth; his eyes pinched tightly.

Clifton peered over his shoulder. The king's guards heaped on top of one another, all dead. King Richard and Henry fenced. The poisoned dart had simply scratched the king's skin, caught in the woven shirt beneath his armor. Clifton wiped his face, spreading Dane's blood over his cheeks.

Jasper knelt beside him. "Here, Clifton. You will need these now." He held out the Arrow of Light and the Bow of Jehu.

Clifton took them, his tears cutting through the smeared blood on his cheeks.

"Ya know what ya have to do, lad," Dane said, his breathing shallow, eyes closed.

"Wake up, Dane!" Clifton said, shaking him hard. The dwarf's eyes shot open. "I won't let you die. Not when I can save you." Clifton reached for the fletching of the Arrow of Light. "The feathers can make you live forever, remember? I can heal you. I can save you, Dane. You don't have to die."

"No, lad," Dane said, taking hold of Clifton's wrist. "You didn't come here to save me." His words came out in short, raspy breaths. He smiled his crooked little grin. "We're both part of something greater than ourselves, you and I."

Clifton wiped his eyes. He didn't want to listen to Dane. He didn't want to choose between the life of his friend and the life of a tyrant king.

And as if hearing his thoughts, Dane looked up into Clifton's eyes and said, "Ya must do what ya were brought here to do." Clifton listened as Dane's breathing slowed. "Farewell, my friend. It has been an honor to have known you."

And Dane closed his eyes for the last time.

Chapter Fifty
The Arrow

"C lifton!" Edward shouted.

The noises of the battlefield returned, flooding his ears, and Clifton looked up. King Richard had his lance outstretched, warring with Henry, whose arms were bloody from the king's blows.

"Clifton," Edward pleaded. "You must help! Please, Clifton—please!"

King Richard struck Henry again and again, hard blows to his chest and sides. The king's face no longer resembled that of a human, but more like the writhing demon haunting Clifton's dreams the night before.

This was the moment. The moment a boy from a different time

and place had been brought here to face. And why? What difference could he possibly make? And then everything became clear. Just like Dane said. It was as if he had been stumbling through darkness ever since he found the arrow, until now, when everything was in the light. And the reason he had been chosen was all he could see.

He was there to make things right.

It wasn't about killing a tyrant king and restoring a throne to its rightful heir; it was about the princes themselves, their story that needed to be told. They would never again feel the love of their mother or the breath of their father, something Clifton would have again if he ever made it home. The princes were forgotten by history, abandoned, and written off as dead. They weren't even buried. He owed them that honor—the place in history stolen from them, along with everything good in their lives.

Clifton raised the stiff bow of Jehu, its humming string burning with a golden-white glow. He notched the Arrow of Light, the fletching swaying as if in an unseen breeze. While he could not save Dane, who had bravely died on the battlefield, Clifton could make sure that his friend had not died in vain. He knew what he had to do, and he was ready. Clifton drew back on the bowstring, aiming like he had done so many times in his own world; only this time, he aimed for a cruel king's heart.

And Clifton released.

Chapter Fifty-One
Long Live the King

Henry lay on the ground unarmed when the Arrow of Light struck King Richard in his unguarded heart. Holding a pole axe in the air, the king gasped and threw his weapon down. His body contorted as the diamond tip struck his thick armor and sliced through to his chest, knocking him onto his back, where the arrow pinned him to the ground. He gripped at it, the tip searing his flesh and the shaft melting deeper still, while Simurgh's feathers in the fletching waved, leeching the king's life. Clifton stared until the light's glow faded, and the feathers lay still. Until the Arrow of Light disintegrated into dust then disappeared.

It was quiet, except for the king's rattling breath. Prince Richard finally stirred from the cannonball explosion. Edward helped him to his feet, placing his arm underneath his brother's shoulders. "Are you all right, Richard?"

"I think so. It hurts, but I can move."

Wobbling as one, they moved across the field to where their uncle lay wounded. The king turned his head slowly to look up at his nephews. They simply stared at each other. Finally, Prince Richard said, "You got what you deserved." And he spit on the dying king before limping away.

Henry wiped his face dry before approaching Edward. All around them, Royal soldiers retreated in droves at the news that King Richard had fallen. Loyalist soldiers found their second wind. The king took in slow, uneven breaths, the ground of Ambion Hill beneath him stained crimson with blood.

"I hope you find peace, Uncle," Edward said. "And I hope it was worth the cost."

King Richard raised his eyes to meet Edward's. He tried speaking to his nephew, but it only came out in a gurgle. Perhaps he wanted to apologize, or maybe gloat. No one would ever know because the king uttered his last breath and died. In silence, they stood around the dead king. Jasper leaned down and closed Richard's eyes, then bowed and stepped off to the side.

Henry clasped Edward on his shoulder. "How do you fair?"

Edward wiped a tear from his eye and nodded. "I feel…justified, somehow, as if a great weight has been lifted from me for generations to come."

"Good, My Lord," Henry said. "These men have battled for your honor. They serve you well." He let go of Edward and turned to Clifton. "And you, Sir Clifton. What a brilliant shot. You have accomplished all that the arrow chose you for."

"Yes," Edward added, moving closer to Clifton. "You have restored back to me what my uncle has stolen. I can never repay you for what you have done."

"It was nothing," Clifton said, his chin dipping down. "I just did what I had to do. I know you'd have done the same, Highness."

Edward smiled. "You are a good friend." He looked back down at his uncle. "I am afraid you cannot take the Arrow of Light back with you. It seems to have disappeared."

"Is that normal?"

"No. The Arrow of Light has existed from Creation. Three others were forged in the beginning but have not been accounted for in many years. This one was the last in existence that I know of. I cannot predict what this turn of events means."

"But now, we must end this war," Henry said, stepping away. He reached the king's royal banner bearer, who lay dead in the field. Henry pried the tightly clutched pike out of his hand and held it high in the air. "King Richard is dead!" he shouted in triumph. "The victory is ours!"

As his voice carried across the field, the Loyalist's cheered one by one. Henry reached his own banner bearer and took the banner from him, running to the base of Ambion Hill, where he threw down the royal banner and stabbed the Loyalist's banner pike in the earth.

"VICTORY!" he bellowed.

His echo spread through the battlefield, and the men cheered, galloping on horses and running toward the hill to meet him. Two soldiers, one Clifton recognized from the ship by the jagged yellow scar on his face, took torches and set the royal banner on fire. The men shouted, arms raised and fists pumping.

Clifton watched as Loyalist soldiers on horseback chased down the king's soldiers trying to flee by foot. He imagined they killed every last one of them.

"It is over now, Uncle," Edward said. "And you have lost." He made the sign of the cross. "May God have mercy on your soul. May you be treated in death as you treated others in life." He removed the gold crown from his head, turned his back, and never looked back.

Clifton and Richard followed Edward to the base of the hill where Henry surveyed the battlefield. Many of his men lay dead. Many more were wounded. Those that could walk, gathered. Edward sidled next to Henry, the crown in his hands.

"Today, a tyrant has been killed, and a crown has been restored," Edward said. "It is with overwhelming grief that I lay my eyes upon so many dead, so many men who made the ultimate sacrifice for righteousness."

Tears welled in Clifton's eyes as he thought of Dane.

"I hold in my hands the crown of the king of England," Edward continued. "And I give it to her true King, Henry Tudor."

Henry's eyes widened as if taken off guard by Edward's decision to freely give him the throne. He bowed, allowing Edward to set the crown on his head, then turned to face his men.

"Long live the king," Edward chanted.

"Long live the king!" the men echoed. "Long live the king!"

Chapter Fifty-Two
Farewell

E lizabeth stood in the doorway of the monastery at Merevale, still wearing the crème colored dress and holding the lace handkerchief. Grief filled her face as the battered men entered through the gates in far less numbers than had left for battle.

The monks brought herbs and basins of water to tend to the soldiers who could be saved. They brought blankets and prayers for the ones who could not.

"Henry," Elizabeth cried as he entered the gate. She ran to him, and they hugged. "I prayed for your protection."

"Thank you, My Lady," Henry said with a wince, his arms and torso bruised. "Your prayers have been answered."

"And my uncle?"

He paused, looking to Edward. "He died on the battlefield with honor, Sister," Edward said. "Now, Henry Tudor rules the throne of England. And you will be his queen." He bowed low.

Elizabeth's mouth dropped open.

Richard hobbled in under Jasper's arm, and Elizabeth moved to meet him, her eyes welled with tears. "Are you all right, Richard?"

"I will be fine, Elizabeth. Do not worry." He forced a smile. "My battle scars will gain me great sympathy from the young courtesans when I return to Èze."

"And you will likely receive more attention than you can handle," Elizabeth said. She scanned the men, her face suddenly worried. "Where is Clifton Chase?"

"Here, My Lady," he said.

She walked over, and Elizabeth hugged him. "Thank you," she whispered, her voice not hiding her tears. "You have brought me all I could ever dream."

He didn't know what to say.

She looked past him to the wall where he had been standing. "Where is your companion, the dwarf?"

A lump grew in his throat, cutting off his air. He could barely speak. "He didn't make it." Fresh tears fell from his eyes. Elizabeth's eyes also filled with tears, and she held Clifton again. They separated as a few soldiers stalked through the gates, balancing a plank carrying Dane's body. Clifton looked away, his tears threatening to overflow again.

"Oh, no," Elizabeth said, her delicate hand covering her mouth.

They set the dwarf in the outdoor atrium on a rock slab where the men gathered around him to pay their respects. Elizabeth wept, wrapped in Henry's arms. Edward and Richard knelt before the stout little man, wiping tears from their eyes. Jasper stepped forward, kissed his fingers, then touched them to Dane's lifeless forehead.

Clifton watched from the wall, knowing if he moved any closer, he would lose it. He spotted a patch of wildflowers growing beside the wall and grabbed a handful. He stood over Dane's body. "Thank you," he whispered, laying the flowers over his chest. "You taught me more than you will ever know."

The monks began to chant.

Jasper Tudor removed Dane's sword. "I will return this to his wife, with honor. She has made a great sacrifice for the kingdom."

Clifton wiped his tears. "I wish I could have saved him."

Edward placed an arm on Clifton's shoulder. "Death comes for us all. But for those who willingly give their lives in sacrifice, they find that in death, they are reborn."

Clifton nodded. His heart ached. He did what he was brought here to do. Now, he simply wanted to go home.

Jasper began singing:

Through darkened nights
the path is worn,
in death a spirit is reborn.
Though tears may fall,
this is the plan,
there is a death for every man.
But do not cry
for day will break,
the morning brings what nighttime takes.
And in this place
we shall not mourn
in death, a spirit is reborn.
In death, a spirit is reborn.

Chapter Fifty-Three
Flight Home

S imurgh landed in the field outside the abbey where Clifton
waited with the others. Clifton turned to Edward and
Richard. "Well, I guess this is good-bye."

"So. it seems," Edward said with a smile. "Thank you for
everything."

"You are the truest of friends," Richard said. "And you shall never be
forgotten."

Henry reached out his hand. "Stay well, Sir Clifton of
Melbourne."

Clifton shook his hand. "You too, Sire."

Henry leaned in close. "I shall be waiting for Columbus to make
his discovery."

"Not for too long. About another seven years."

Jasper stepped forward. "Your bow, Clifton Chase." He held

bow of Jehu in his outstretched palms, his head low.

"Thanks, Jasper. Thanks for everything."

Jasper nodded and took a step back.

Elizabeth hugged Clifton. "Good-bye, my friend. You have brought me back all that was taken from me."

Clifton bowed. "A pleasure, My Lady."

Clifton stepped toward Simurgh, then turned to see his friends lined up to watch him go. "Well, good-bye," he said again, climbing upon Simurgh's broad back. Her feathers warmed his hands.

"Farewell," Edward said, as Simurgh lifted into the air.

"Good-bye," Clifton called down, waving, watching until he flew so high that his friends disappeared into the colors of the green fields and brown mountains.

Simurgh flew above the white clouds to the expanse of blue sky high above. "You have done well," she said. "The arrow chose wisely."

Clifton's eyes grew heavy, the soft feathers comforting and familiar, like an old blanket. Simurgh's warm body felt strong and firm, like his mattress.

"Thank you, Simurgh."

"And now you return to your world, with the knowledge you have gained from this one."

"Yeah, I guess I have learned a lot," Clifton said, yawning. "But I have one question. Why weren't you there to fight? We could've used your help."

"I told you before; this task was yours to fulfill. But you would always have my broad back to carry you. Have I not kept my word?"

Clifton nodded, his eyes drooping. "But what about Dane? You could've saved him. Why didn't you?"

"Dane's path was chosen by the Creator before the foundation of the earth was laid. That is true for all of us. No one can interfere with what has already been preordained."

"But I kind of did that, didn't I? By saving the princes and putting things back?"

"You did nothing more than what you were supposed to do."

"But didn't I change the future?"

"But didn't I change the future?"

"For one, yes."

"Who?"

"I cannot give you your answers, Clifton. My purpose is to give you the wisdom to find your own answers."

He thought about it for some time, as the cold wind rattled through his hair and the clouds changed into a sheer mist that he couldn't see through. "It's me, isn't it? The one whose future changed."

"Do you feel like you have changed?"

Clifton thought about all that had happened to him since he found the Arrow of Light. He barely knew the kid who had found the strange arrow in his closet, even though it had only been a few days ago. Or was it weeks? He couldn't tell anymore. "Yeah, I guess I have changed."

"Then you have all your answers. But for now, sleep, child. You will be home very soon."

Chapter Fifty-Four

The Arrow of Light

C lifton opened his eyes to a dark room. He was lying on a soft bed, one which he recognized. Pictures he remembered nailing up hung on the walls. His backpack sat on the floor. A candle burned on his desk.

He was home.

Could it have been just a dream? An adventure he had made up in his head? He hoped not. He hoped his friends in England were real, just as much as he hoped he was real to his friends in England. But part of him didn't even care. He wanted to see his family.

Someone knocked on the door, and Clifton propped up onto his elbows. The handle turned, and his mom stepped in.

"Mom!" Clifton said, jumping up to hug her. "I was afraid I'd never see you again."

She looked puzzled. "What are you talking about? I brought your dinner just a half an hour ago. Are you feeling okay, sweetie?"

"I feel great. Where's dad? Is he here?"

"In the kitchen, but—"

Clifton shot past her, then ran back to her and kissed her on the cheek. "I'm sorry I was such a pain. I love you so much."

"Apology accepted."

Clifton sprinted to the kitchen, sliding in his tube socks down the hall. His dad sat at the kitchen table reading the newspaper. Clifton stopped in the doorway. "Dad?"

His dad looked up. He caught Clifton's eyes and furrowed his brow, looking back down at his newspaper. "You done with those letters already?" he said.

"Dad, I never should have said those things. And I never should have fought at school."

His dad looked up; his eyebrows raised in disbelief.

"Sometimes, I forget what's really important," Clifton continued, "and I forget that it's not all about me. I'm really sorry."

His dad stared at him, speechless.

Clifton walked over and hugged him. "I love you, Dad."

"I love you, too, son." They pulled away from each other. "I'm sorry, too."

Clifton sat across from him at the table. His dad smiled and said, "It's easy to lose sight of what's important. But it seems to me that you've figured out what's most important in life. I'm proud of you."

"Thanks, Dad."

Clifton's mom stood in the doorway. His dad nodded at her, and she disappeared.

"Your mother and I have been waiting a long time to give you something very special. We couldn't let you have it until you proved you were mature enough to take care of it."

Clifton's mom came back into the doorway, smiling. Her soft smile reminded him of Liv. Suddenly, his heart ached.

His dad stood and put his arm around Clifton's shoulder. "Come here, son."

They entered the living room, where Pierce sat on the floor, playing with trucks. He flashed Clifton a huge smile. Clifton smiled back, beyond happy to be home.

"After what you've said," his dad continued, "I think you have proven you are ready."

On the couch sat a quiver with a few arrows, each fletching made of copper-colored feathers.

"They were your great-grandpa's set. And I think he would have wanted you to have them."

"Congratulations," his mom said.

Clifton slid one of the arrows out of the quiver. The tip was like a diamond. He ran his fingers between the barbs of the feathers, which seemed to be moving, but barely, and he smiled. When the light hit the smooth wood, for a quick second, like a flashlight turning on and off really quickly, he swore the shaft glowed, exactly like the Arrow of Light.

But this time, there were three of them.

Chapter Fifty-Five
The Boy and the Girl

C lifton closed his locker after the last bell. He had spent the past week learning all that he could about his great-grandpa. His name was Ezekiel Clifton Chase, and he had thirteen children, Clifton's grandfather being the youngest. He was actually a sheriff in the western frontier in the late 1800s. Clifton still hadn't figured out where he got the arrows from. And none of them had glowed again since his parents had first given them to him. But what if?

As he walked down the hall, Clifton heard his name called out.

"Chase!"

Clifton turned. It was Ryan Rivales. A crowd gathered, hoping for the fight that had started in the gym but never finished.

"What do you want, Ryan

Ryan snickered, mimicking Clifton's voice while repeating,

"What do you want, Ryan?" Three kids standing beside him laughed.

"I don't want to fight you, man." He turned and walked away. Ava came around the corner with Justin, and they both stopped.

"Where you going, Chase? I was talking to you," Ryan hollered, gaining even more rubberneckers for his showdown.

Clifton looked into Ava's eyes and gave her the most reassuring smile he could muster. He faced Ryan. "Were you? Cause it sounded like you were trying to look tough in front of all your friends."

The crowd *oohed* and *awed*. This was not going the way Clifton planned.

"Look, I've got nothing against you, Ryan. I just want to be left alone." Clifton turned to leave again, but Ryan shoved him in the back, knocking him to the ground.

Ava gasped and covered her mouth.

It's now or never, Clifton thought, pushing himself back to his feet. Ryan's wide smile was devious. Clifton shook his head. "Dude, what's the matter with you? Why are you so against making friends?"

"I've got plenty of friends," Ryan said, waving at the crowd gathered around him.

Clifton shook his head. "These guys aren't your friends. They're afraid of you, or they want to watch you cause a scene. Do you think any of them would be there for you if you really needed them or would they be the first to turn you in to save their skin? They don't care about you, Ryan."

"What did you say?"

"I'm saying for a guy who has been to as many schools as you; I'd think maybe you would try to make some real friends. There are a lot of good people out there who could have your back when you need them to." He faced Justin, who was nodding at him. "Maybe I could have been a good friend for you if I hadn't been so busy trying to impress people." He looked over at Ava who was beaming.

Clifton picked his backpack off the floor and strapped it on. "I kind of feel sorry for you. It's gotta be hard having to leave your home and everything you know."

Ryan said, "Is there something you wanna say to me?"

Clifton huffed. "Yeah. I guess what I'm trying to say is I'm sorry for being a jerk. I'm sorry for not trying to see the world through your eyes from the beginning."

Ryan shook his head. "What? Are you serious? Hey," he said to the crowd, "get a load of Chase trying to have a bromance moment." He laughed, and so did the three punks standing around him. But the rest of the crowd slowly dispersed.

"Later, Ryan." Clifton continued down the hall.

"I'm not finished with you!" Ryan shouted, marching forward.

"Oh yes, you are," said Coach Alonso, who held Ryan's arm in a tight grip. "That's detention for starting a fight on school grounds. And if I were you, I'd strongly consider those wise words Mr. Chase freely gave you. Friends like that are hard to find, and I bet you could use a few good friends." He gave Clifton a wink as he dragged Ryan away.

The look on Ryan's face was classic.

Clifton climbed down the steps of the front walkway; a huge grin plastered across his face.

"Clifton!"

He turned around. Ava was running up beside him, her blonde hair catching the sunlight. "You were really great in there."

"Thanks."

She crinkled her nose. "You seem… different, somehow."

"I feel different."

They both smiled and let out a nervous laugh. An awkward silence followed. Clifton stared at her a second too long, and she caught his eyes.

"What?" she asked.

"You know who you look like?"

"No," she said. "Who?"

"Elizabeth Tudor."

"Whose she?"

"She's a girl who lived a long time ago. She was extremely brave. And very… beautiful."

Ava's cheeks blushed rose.

"If you'd like, I can walk you home and tell you about her. I mean, if you want."

"Sure," Ava said. "I'd like that."

The End

If you enjoyed this book, please take a moment to review for other readers to discover it.

Become a fan @theWRITEengle

ACKNOWLEDGMENTS

So many people went into the making of this book, and I couldn't have done it without all of them. In no particular order, I'd like to thank my critique group for your honest and sometimes brutal suggestions (John, Bill, Mark, Dean, Jeremy, Christine, and Ryan); to Jim for helping me perfect the many drafts; to Christine for more coffee and friendship, and your constant ear; to Kitt and the 5th and 6th grade FPS students 2011-2012, and the 3rd graders 2012-2013 at Suntree Elementary School for listening and loving Clifton before anyone else; to Kammie for Clifton's last name; to Clara for reading the entire manuscript first; to Debbie for putting the perfect pictures to my words; to my beta readers; to the four agents who rejected Clifton and gave me amazing feedback; to my children for bragging about me to their friends; to my parents; to my husband for letting me labor over a manuscript instead of getting a day job and always providing me with unconditional love and support; to the SCBWI, especially Linda, for the conferences, resources, and guidance; to God for gifting me with this talent that I will not bury; to me—that's right, to myself, for never giving up, no matter how hard, how scary, or how many no's I faced; and finally, to you—the reader of this book, who took a chance on me. I hope you found yourself lost in the story, and in many more to come.

FROM THE AUTHOR

Bullying is a real issue, and you can help by remembering:
Your words have power!

You can speak life into others by building them up, or you can destroy them with what you say. Always remember the Golden Rule, and that sometimes, you must be the voice for someone who can't speak for themselves. **Stand up for yourself and others by using your powerful words to fight bullying!**

ABOUT THE AUTHOR

Jaimie Engle has been writing since she was seven years old. The idea for Clifton Chase was inspired by a real-life oil painting depicting the Battle of Bosworth Field, the same painting she included in Clifton's story. She lives in Florida, just near Wickham Park, with her husband, youngest son, and a hound dog.

Visit her at www.thewriteengle.com

ABOUT THE ILLUSTRATOR

Debbie Waldorf Johnson worked over 25 years in graphic design and spent a few more years painting and teaching watercolor. She has won several awards for her watercolor paintings. As a grandmother, Debbie enjoys creating images for her grandchildren, picture books, and commercial publications. She lives near the ocean with her husband, Ken, in Melbourne, Florida, where they love getting a little sand between their toes.

Visit her at www.Debbiejohnsonartist.wordpress.com.

Read on for the exciting sequel to
Clifton Chase The Arrow of Light by Jaimie Engle.

Clifton Chase

on

Castle Rock

Jaimie Engle

PART ONE: THE BOY

Chapter One

T here is no way to know, when the day starts like any other, that something extraordinary is on the horizon. On a normal morning in a small town, Clifton Chase opened his eyes. He got dressed in jean shorts and a T-from a summer camp several years earlier, then walked to the kitchen to pour a bowl of cereal. It was March in Florida, and he had no reason to think anything was out of the ordinary. No warning by an outside source, no peculiar crunch in his breakfast cereal to suggest he move more cautiously on this particular day. In fact, it started in the normal mundane way that any other morning starts.

And Clifton was glad.

"Clifton," his mother called from her bedroom. "We're leaving for archery club in five minutes."

"That's today?" he called back.

"Yes, and we're running late."

Clifton slurped his milk and placed his dish in the sink. Skidding down the hardwood floor hallway in tube socks, he reached his bedroom door and rushed in. A stained oak bed with matching dresser, end table, and a growing collection of medieval relics littered the room, including a miner's pedestal lantern converted to an electric lamp, and a board with a grouping of hilts and pommels, from where he hung his backpack and jackets.

Clifton swung open his closet door which squeaked at the hinges. He reached for his chucks but stopped. Beside the bookcase packed with board games and novels, wedged behind his art supplies and science equipment, the copper feather caught his attention, a feather he was certain had not been there when he put his sneakers away the night before.

He had placed the three arrows with copper feathers that his parents had given him in the far back of his closet where he couldn't see them or touch them. Where he could forget how the first arrow had brought him through time to 1485 England to rescue two princes from their tyrant uncle, fight in an epic battle, and watch his good friend, a dwarf named Dane, die before his eyes. No, Clifton was hoping to get back to normal, trying to pretend the adventure never happened, knowing deep down it very well had.

He passed his fingers through the barbs of the fletching. It felt like the feathers that found their way to his front porch from nearby nesting birds, but in a shade of copper flecked with golden shimmers he'd never seen on any birds in Melbourne. The wood shaft was made from the Tree of Knowledge, where Simurgh, the all-knowing bird of reason nested before Time herself existed on Earth. He knew these things, but he wanted to forget them. He was chosen by the Arrow of Light in the past to be the voice for those who couldn't. While he had accomplished this task, it wasn't one he wished to repeat. Unless, he could see Pearl again, the beautiful young Siren who had rescued him from an evil Mer King. At the thought of Pearl, the lightweight shaft heated up in his hand, the light brightened, the fletching shimmered.

Then, at the rear of the closet, he thought he saw a pair of eyes glowing in the dark spaces between his clothes. He blinked hard and shook his head. When he shifted, something in his closet caught the light for the slightest second. It jutted out like a witch's nose. He leaned in for a closer look. Someone else was in his closet. He reached out to touch it, but it was only the hanger angled in such a way to force his fear to paint pictures.

Clifton went to step back, but the arrow caught on something then released, the force knocking him into his board games, which toppled to the floor. Pieces flew across the rug. Clifton smacked the floor at the base of his bookshelf. Someone else was definitely in his closet.

He stood, his pulse racing, and flung his hanging clothes to the side, finding nothing. He ran his fingers through his hair. What was the matter with him? But he knew. The Arrows of Light were magical, and many beings would go through great lengths to find them for their own gain. No matter how desperately Clifton wished life would be normal again, he knew as long as he possessed the arrows, it never would.

Suddenly, he got that feeling again that he wasn't alone, like someone was tip toeing behind him. Clifton jolted around half-expecting to catch the glowing eyed monster snooping around but found nothing out of the ordinary. Quite normal, actually.

"Clifton, it's time to go, now," his mother said from the hall outside his door.

"Okay, Mom. I'm coming."

He put the arrow in the back of his closet with the other two and threw on his shoes without tying them, still unable to shake the feeling that he *was* being watched. And the glowing eyes in the closet he couldn't quite see, closed tight, shadowing the creature in darkness.

Coming, Fall of 2020 to INtense Publications…

CPSIA information can be obtained
at www.ICGtesting.com
Printed in the USA
LVHW042036181219
641009LV00001B/35/P